Gellert's New Job

Johannes T. Evans

Gellert has worked as a business manager for the King family for nearly a decade when an error in judgement brings his employment to an abrupt end. Lucien Pike, a rival kingpin, employs his services instead.

Fantasy, crime, and a good bit of dark humour. 21k. Rated M. Transgender, autistic man's POV; both protagonists are autistic.

Content warnings: depictions of violence, blood, sexual harassment including assault, pregnancy and fetishism of pregnancy, misogyny, biting; discussions of and reference to transphobia, ableism, past sexual trauma, child abuse including child sexual abuse and ABA, child neglect.

Gellert's New Job is a work of fiction created from the author's imagination. Any resemblance to living persons, living or dead, or resemblance to actual events, places, or names is purely coincidental.

Gellert's New Job

Lashton was a smuggling town.

Once upon a time, it had been a village, a handful of houses and a pub at the end of the peninsula where the fishing was good. Lashton itself had been all humans, but swathed as it was in the magical mists that came in on the eastern winds, they'd mostly been a magical lot, and had lived side by side with the fae villages on the closest coast.

That had been a long, long time ago.

What had been Lashton once had grown back and back into the peninsula, meeting the coast, so that Greater Lashton was separated from the Little Lashton it had spawned, and the peninsula's spoon had been built on so it went farther and farther out into the water, bits of Greater Lashton being built higher and higher, on stilts, in towers.

It had grown so big that Greater Lashton and Little Lashton had become one thing again, and the other villages had been subsumed into its borders — the whole bay together was Lashton now.

It was only spite and notions of humility that stopped the residents calling it a city.

It didn't resemble what it had used to on a map, an eyelash on the rounded eye formed by the coast: houses were built all over now, into cliffsides, on top of one another, in tight rows, and every street was labyrinthine with all the buildings stuffed tight together. Walking down one street you'd see secret alleys that led impossible distances, from one end of the bay to the other in five steps, and there wasn't a Lashton resident that couldn't count off five shortcuts for each finger they had.

Long bridges of heavy wood logs formed bridges between the peninsula's end and the northern coast of the bay, each of them enchanted to stick loosely together like magnet strips, and they rose and fell with the waves.

It was a genuinely mixed town, not like the fae-human ones with clearly separated neighbourhoods and borders within. There were barely any *official* borders in Lashton — they'd be too hard to draw — only businesses and homes that ran one way or the another.

And they *had* to run one way or another, or else.

Smuggling was a way of life in Lashton, and in absence of loyalty to the Crown, one had to have loyalty to other factions.

Everyone you knew smuggled one thing or another past the watchful eye of the Crown's Royalty and Customs Service, whether it was something as exciting as pixie dust (a popular name for an extremely addictive hallucinogen made from powdered fae mushrooms) or something as routine as a Breton toffee too similar to a Welsh product of a suspiciously similar name — but better tasting all around.

Tunnels ran all over, in and out of Lashton, some of them going so far you could go underground on the beach and come out again in the middle of the Llallwg National Forest fifty miles north, others letting you come up on magical islands out in the English Channel. Some pocket dimensions had been set up *just* for smuggling, so that you'd slip through a magical door and end up in some liminal space with crates piled up on every side, and be lucky to find your way out again.

This was the town that Gellert Osgodby had lived in almost all his life, and he didn't think he'd ever leave it, not for good.

He'd gone to university, gotten his degree, but that had been more than enough of the world outside Lashton for him — he missed its mismatched streets and strange pathways, missed the noise and bustle in the streets, missed being able to tell someone's loyalties at a glance, and act accordingly.

He had hardened to survive under Lashton's harsh ways — outside its borders, he no longer fit.

It hadn't been difficult to find a job when he'd come home, of course, as there were always openings for a good accountant in Lashton.

He'd gone from one place to another for a while, cooking the books for different businesses and seeing what suited him, and it had been eight years ago now that Dandy King had approached him about managing the wholesaler's, King & Co., on Draig Street. He'd not even been twenty-five when he'd taken the role, but he had grown with it and into it, and he was good at what he did.

On the day this employment came to an end, it was a wet and drizzly day outside, water filtering into the troughs and gaps in the mismatched cobbled streets, and Gellert had been putting out fires all day.

First, a shipment coming up from London had gone missing somewhere in Lincolnshire. This, in itself, would not have been an issue, as it was mostly clothes for the new season — of course, in actuality, it was absolutely an issue, as hidden inside the bales were several bricks of pixie dust, and the Kings had already been nervous of late, what with the Pikes founding a new factory nearby for the stuff, with no travel needed at all.

The other issues weren't issues because they were big, but because they were numerous, in order:

· Courageous King had broken his femur in a climbing accident, and this meant that Dandy and a good many of the other Kings were dealing with the infighting that resulted in the aftermath. Gellert, who had seen Courageous King fail to scale steps, let alone a cliffside, was privately of the opinion that the likely orchestrator of this injury was Courageous himself, but the Kings would not be Kings if they did not assume an assassination attempt.

· The Pikes had started the aforementioned new factory for pixie dust somewhere within Lashton's limits, and everyone was doing their best to find precisely where it was and how to replicate its efficiency of production, including outsiders from Lashton itself.

· There was a property dispute becoming increasingly violent on the southside of town, which meant that many shipments within Lashton's limits were either lost or being held hostage out that way.

· The cops had arrested a chapter of one of the other families, which was a drama in itself, but involved in the same arrest were several people that were supposedly rivalling with the arrestees in question, prompting rumours of either informants or betrayal.

· Word had it that a favourite pocket watch of a very high-ranking King had been seen on the streets, sold almost for scrap, and for the Kings, who took watches very seriously, this was a personal insult for reasons more than the theft itself.

Control of Lashton was primarily divided between five families, these being the Kings, the Laithes, the Renns, the Sorrels, and the Pikes, and as much as days like this were hard, the clear delineation of these families and their loyalties was a comforting balm. Every house and business had its ownership, its loyalties, to one of the big families or some smaller faction, and Gellert liked that.

It was predictable, clean, easy — violent, yes, but so long as you could hold your own, and presented no easy target, so long as you followed the rules, you could play family loyalties against one another, could dip in and out of almost any trouble.

Gellert had always felt himself adept at this until that afternoon, and later, it was himself that he blamed.

His phone had been constantly buzzing in his pocket the day through, computer awash with emails, not to mention the various messengers that kept bringing notes in person or by spell arrow; the cashier, Tobey, was filling in for Fanciful King, and he was sweating so profusely with the anxiety that Gellert had made him mop twice, and the clerk with whom Gellert shared the office had been on the verge of conniption the day through.

This was all before Dai Laithe strode through the doors holding a wooden crate in his hand, and set it down on the counter.

Gellert didn't hear what passed between Laithe and young Tobey initially, watching from behind the glass walls of the office on the next floor, but he did see the way Tobey crumpled inward, the way he physically shrank away and trembled, more sweat dripping onto the vinyl floor.

Gellert kept his head high as he went downstairs.

"How can we help you, Mr Laithe?" he asked coolly, and Dai turned to look at him.

Dai Laithe was not a big man, but he was young and desperate to prove himself — he was only a head taller than Gellert, not even six feet, and he was thinner than Gellert was, built like a sapling tree with spindly arms and a narrow waist. He tried to make himself look bigger, faced with Gellert's sharp glare from behind the thick bottle glass of his spectacles, but Gellert had faced far bigger men than him, and it did not have the effect he suspected Dai desired.

"Parcel," he said, gesturing.

"Yes, I see that," said Gellert. "What has it to do with us?"

"You're looking after it," said Dai. Had he stopped there, perhaps Gellert might have kept his temper — perhaps he might have arched an eyebrow, said something catty, checked in with one of the other Laithes, received a proper explanation, and set it aside. The Kings and the Laithes did do favours for one another from time to time, after all. Unfortunately, Dai did not stop there. Faced with Gellert's scowling expression, he squared his almost non-existent shoulders even more, leaning over to look down at him, and said, "And if you know what's good for you, you'll put it right aside. Speccy little cunt."

He didn't spit on the floor, but the spit was heavily implied, and Gellert felt his veins burn abruptly hot with angry blood.

He didn't let his face change, but he heard Tobey's frightened gasp, and this made Dai's mask of haughty confidence falter, revealing the anxiety underneath. He and Gellert had had no direct interactions before now, but Dai must have known enough about him to be frightened.

"Of course," he said smoothly, forcing out the brittle edge as he picked up the crate by its handles. "Come with me, Mr Laithe, and I'll show you precisely where we'll set it aside for you."

Dai's hesitation faded, and he puffed himself up as though inflated, striding behind Gellert as he strode with the crate back toward the door.

"It needs to be dry," said Dai, with a bare smidge of audible uncertainty.

"Does it?" asked Gellert, balancing the crate on his hip as he opened the door again with a cheerful jingle of the entry bell.

"What the fuck are you —"

When Gellert tossed the crate down the steps and onto the cobbled stones at the bottom of them, it came apart very dramatically, sending glass baubles of what looked to be some sort of enhancement potion rattling down the sloping street — those that didn't shatter immediately, that was, and stain the muddy puddles in technicolour.

Dai looked at him in utter fury, and advanced.

"You can't fucking —"

Gellert tripped him on the top stair, giving Dai a hard shove in the back and sending him sailing down the same way his merchandise had.

He heard the satisfying splash just before he slammed the door shut.

Tobey and the clerk were both staring at him.

"Cover the cash desk for Tobey for half an hour, would you, Eddie? Let him have a sit down and a cup of tea," said Gellert. "And mop that floor again."

Through the twitched blind of the door, he could see Dai Laithe dragging himself awkwardly to his feet, his skinny suit and carefully styled hair stained with mud and coloured dye and a little blood — there was a group of kids his age or a little younger, seventeen or eighteen, laughing at him.

He should have known it would be a problem then.

Perhaps, in a way, he did.

* * *

He hadn't been expecting Dandy King to be waiting for him in his office when he came into work the next morning, but nor did he find himself surprised to see him. Gellert had had his reactivity trained out of him at a very, very young age.

Dandy was leaning back in Gellert's ergonomic chair, his elbows on the arms, one leg crossed loosely over the other. He was everything that Dai Laithe wanted to encompass, Gellert suspected, with his skinny style and coiffed hair: sleek, graceful, and really quite frightening.

"Gellert," said Dandy softly, swinging his pocket watch by the chain from his fingers, and idly watching it spin when he plucked on the little golden links. This was a habit of his, when he was intimidating someone — Gellert might take it to heart, were it not for the fact that he knew he never did this when left to his own devices, that it was purely pageantry. "We're friends, you and I, aren't we?"

"No, Mr King," said Gellert bluntly, and Dandy's eyes flitted up even as his watch spun on air. "You are my employer, and I your employee."

"Eight years, Gellert," said Dandy, eyes narrowing slightly, "and you don't consider us friends?"

"No," said Gellert. "A friendship is not formed merely by time and proximity, Mr King. You are not my friend, nor I yours."

Dandy cleared his throat, sitting forward in the chair and pulling his watch up into his hand.

They were the same age, he and Gellert — they hadn't gone to school together, of course, because the Kings were far too good for the school Gellert had gone to, but Gellert was always aware of their similar ages at times like these, when Dandy was leveraging his power over him.

He didn't enjoy it, when it was Gellert — it was part of what made Gellert such a capable manager of his business, but on a personal level, Dandy missed having his ego stroked by a littler man's fear.

"I suppose that makes this easier, then," said Dandy. "Tell me what happened with Dai Laithe."

"He demanded we hold a parcel for him, after insulting and intimidating young Tobey — and then attempting to insult and intimidate me. Young Mr Laithe disrespected your business, Mr King, and you, by extension. Won't you forgive me for taking offence?"

Dandy huffed out a single laugh: it was a surprisingly cold sound, disbelieving, as he shook his head slightly from side to side, but his smile remained.

"See, that's why I hired you, Gellert," he said. "You've got a head for numbers, but you won't be intimidated either, and you know how to turn a situation around on your tongue — it's a good face on the business, keeps people from taking the piss. Thing is, in this case, you *should* have let him take the piss. Why the fuck didn't you get onto Dag and check, 'stead of losing your wick like that?"

"His bluster offended, as I said, and I didn't exactly want to reward him for it."

"Tobey said he called you a speccy little cunt."

"I won't deny that was a contributing factor."

"Gellert."

"Mr King."

"You *are* a speccy little cunt."

Gellert arched one eyebrow, tilting his head slightly to one side. "Did I say I wasn't?"

"I like you, Gellert," said Dandy. "Which is why I'm not going to hurt you."

"Kind of you," said Gellert, although not without a certain hesitation, and he watched cautiously as Dandy stood to his feet, picking up a wooden box and a bottle of black liquid. "Some form of restitution was demanded, I expect."

"We came to an arrangement," said Dandy, and uncorked the bottle. The tar smelt like burning rubber, thick and bubbling in its bottle, and Gellert distantly recalled seeing someone else tarred and feathered at school, remembered the plasticky sensation of the tar, the way it stuck and clung to the hands, ruined the clothes.

The girl had had to get a haircut after, her hair was so ruined by it, and she'd had to scrub herself so hard with a bristled brush to get it loose that she was red raw from head to toe for a week.

"No," said Gellert.

"Oh, don't be like that," said Dandy. "We won't even strip you for it — I know that that sort of thing hits different, being... what you are."

Gellert's scowl deepened.

"Just a bit of embarrassment, that's all," said Dandy kindly, lifting the bottle, "and then we can put all this behind us."

He lowered his arm very quickly when Gellert drove the blade of his flick knife into the joint of his shoulder, and the bottle shattered on the floor. Over the furious sound of Dandy swearing as Gellert dragged his knife back, he had to raise his voice.

"You might consider this my resignation, Mr King," said Gellert, picking his bag back up, and took his leave.

Dandy was still cursing sharply as Gellert turned on his heel and swiftly descended the stairs, and he took the side exit to keep from meeting Dandy's guard at the front door: rushing forward, he slipped first through one false window and then into the back door of the butcher's, following its corridor until he came out beside the florist's two streets over, and took to the main street.

He had already plotted four routes back to his flat by the time his feet hit the cobbles, but it didn't end up mattering — he was surrounded by men on all sides, and instinct took over.

His briefcase dropped to the ground, and Gellert raised his fists.

* * *

By the time the car rolled to a stop, Gellert's mouth was dry around the makeshift gag, and his shoulders were sore from how tightly bound his wrists were, stuck fast against the small of his back. His wrists hurt, his fingers both bruised and cramped, and his mouth still tasted like another man's blood: when they let him out of the car, he stumbled, and had to be pulled up from his knees.

Even not walking steadily, he was aware he didn't immediately recognise the path he was dragged up: it was unfamiliar concrete, new, a pavement, and then cheap concrete slabs. He could hear their hollow sound as all their feet moved over them, hear them creak, until a door opened up ahead.

He inhaled as best he could, trying to take in the smells around him through the sack over his head, but all he could take in was grass.

The door was rickety and loose on its hinges, and the hall it opened into was floored in old, cheap laminate that was loose on the floor, peeling up in places. Even not being able to see it, he could feel that, feel the way it moved with his feet if he shuffled.

The floor inside the little entrance hall was older, felt heavier, a more old-fashioned tile — a heavier vinyl, more firmly adhered in its place.

Although his were quiet, the other men's footsteps — three of them, the huge man dragging him forward by the scruff of his jacket and the two shorter men behind him — were loud, echoing off the narrow halls and high ceiling.

There were a lot of open doors, leading off from the corridor.

Gellert was pulled into one on the left, made to stumble again by the force of the tug, and he shuffled his feet experimentally on the carpet, which was thin but plush — it didn't feel threadbare or worn, but new.

In the corridor there'd been a faintly medical smell of antiseptic mixed with old paper, but it was different in here: he could smell the flowers, not the powdery scent of fresh ones, nor the choking, concentrated scent of perfume or potpourri, but something subtler, rosewater maybe, or a mild floral soap.

This room had a high ceiling too, but the plush surfaces muffled the sound — there was more than the carpet, then, probably heavy wallpaper, curtains, thick furniture.

"Is that him?" asked a deep, slow voice, not one he'd heard before — he had a Cockney accent, not a local one, and Gellert could tell he was in front of him, not standing, but sitting down — that, or he was on the short side.

The big man behind him was to his right, and the other two were standing off to the side, to his left, but there were no new people, no one he could hear.

"Yeah," says one of the smaller men. "You want us to stay?"

"No, you two go. Yves, wait in the hall."

Footsteps, then, the two smaller men walking to leave, and the big man went to follow them, but the man sitting down said, "Yves," in a half-scolding voice.

The sack was pulled from over his head, and he expected the sudden light to hurt, but it was dimmer than expected.

The room was red and rosy, and whatever light there was flickered — a candle, he thought. Was that the smell?

He sighed, irritably, at the reddened blur.

"Yves," said the deep voice. "A gag?"

"He was calling us names," said Yves.

"Yeah, I'm sure he fucking was. Take it off."

The big man had learned his lesson from earlier: he was careful to keep his hands well free of Gellert's mouth this time, and he was too tall to headbutt. Gellert experimentally moved his jaw, and when a straw was put to his mouth he drank the water, felt it wash over his dry tongue and teeth, so that he wasn't tasting Yves' blood anymore.

"The wrists too," said the man.

"I'll wait outside," said Yves: he cut the zip ties in one movement and was out of the door with the next, the door clicking loudly shut.

Gellert was aware of the sound of his own breathing and the heavy beat of his heart in his throat, but without him speaking, he couldn't hear the other man, couldn't tell where he was. Suffice it to say, he was fairly certain that the man in front of him was not one of the Kings —

he hadn't been introduced to the vast majority of the family, but he knew enough of the Kings and the Laithes both to know them by sight, or at least, by ear, and none of them were Londoners.

Gellert massaged his wrists.

"Sorry about all this," said the man.

"You're not," said Gellert softly. "You will be."

"Wanted to speak with you privately, din't I?" said the man, and Gellert carefully catalogued the cues in his accent, the open-mouthed vowel sound, the *th* that became a *v*, the way that *didn't* became *din't*. "No interruptions." No dental t-sound, just a glottal stop.

"So naturally, you kidnapped me," said Gellert. "As one does."

"You talk posh for a Yorkshire lad," said the man. "Your accent don't match what you say."

"And you talk like a hard nut in a cartoon," said Gellert. "I suppose we're both laughable, when you look at it that way."

"There's a lot of potential interruptions already," said the man. "Seems I could get stuck talking with you."

"Instead of killing me or torturing me? Please, talk all you like."

"Who says I'm gonna do that?"

"A little thing we here up north call *common sense.*"

"Oh, I've heard of that," said the man, standing to his feet with a creak of his chair. "Don't like it."

Gellert couldn't see him. The room was a red blur, and he thought the man was tall because his voice was coming from higher up now that he was standing, but he was too far away in the dim, warm light to even make out his silhouette.

"I wanted to hire you," he said.

"No," said Gellert. "Will that be all?"

The carpet was new, but the boards underneath weren't, and when the other man moved forward, Gellert could hear some of them creak under his weight, a few of them rattling in their places.

He moved closer, and Gellert could see that he *was* big — it was hard to tell precisely, but Gellert was fairly certain that his captor might be the same size as Yves, if not bigger.

He was wearing all black, and once he stood directly in front of Gellert, he could see his silhouette, see the blobs of colour that made up his pale face, his pale but darker hair. He was — *big*.

"Do you know who I am?" asked the man in a very quiet voice.

"Should I?" asked Gellert.

The man's hand wrapped around his throat.

He didn't need any further provocation, even though the man barely squeezed: he slipped his knife back out of his pocket, flicked it open, and drove it into the centre of his captor's chest — or, he tried.

The blade glanced off, scraping down the side of his thumb, and he hissed, dropping the knife.

It thudded almost silently against the ground, and the big hand squeezed tighter until he choked, trying to grab at the wrist, which was big enough that both of his hands had trouble wrapping around it.

"Yeah, seems like you don't," he murmured, sounding amused, and dragged Gellert against his chest.

Gellert tried to struggle, tried to kick, but the man was impossibly strong, and when Gellert stamped on his foot he didn't even flinch, his hand squeezing tighter. The hand was very, very cold.

So was the man. Even pulled as close as he was, Gellert couldn't feel his heartbeat, as much as he could hear him breathing — a vampire, then.

"I don't want to kill you," he said. "Just wanna employ your services."

"I don't care," said Gellert, resigned. "Kill me."

"You lost your job today."

"You needn't tell me things I don't know."

"Doing you a favour, in't I? No one else will hire you."

"I'll *move*," Gellert spat, trying to lift himself up on his toes and out of the hand around his throat, but the vampire's hand just went higher with him.

"What about your mum?" asked his captor, squeezing his throat with cool, stiff fingers. "Will you move her too, to a different hospital?"

Gellert's blood went almost as cold as the vampire's was. "You've been stalking me."

The man made a dismissive noise. "Not personally. Got people for that, an't I?"

"What do you want me for?"

"Secretary."

"I'm not a *secretary.*"

"You are now," he said. "Either a secretary or a corpse."

"Who *are* you?"

"You really don't know, do ya?"

"Should I?"

His head was being pulled slightly to the side, and as sharp teeth slid over his neck, he tried not to react as they threatened to cut. His heart was pounding now, and he was distantly aware — although he tried not to be curious — that the mouth threating his throat was a little warmer than the outside, but still not as hot-blooded as Gellert himself.

The teeth were threatening to cut, and he clenched his jaw to keep from giving the satisfaction of a whimper.

"You been bitten before?"

"Is that what you want? A blood cow?"

"*Told* you, I want a secretary. I heard you're good." His tongue slid over the surface of Gellert's neck, as wet and smooth as a human's tongue but oddly cold, and Gellert heaved in a gasping, shuddering breath. "My name is Lucien Pike."

Gellert felt his eyes go wide, but like a deer frozen in headlights, he found he couldn't move.

"Heh," said the vampire. "You know who I am now, don'tcha?"

"Yes," whispered Gellert.

"Good," said Pike, and bit.

Gellert had been bitten before, as it so happened, but only once, and only by a vampire his age when he was still at school, him curious about what her venom felt like, her wanting to know what blood tasted like, fresh from the source. The two of them couldn't have been older than twelve.

Lucien Pike was centuries old: it wasn't the same thing at all.

The pinprick of the teeth piercing the skin was a sharp, momentary pain, and then Pike drew his teeth back to drink, lapping at the fresh wounds. Gellert felt like he was drowning in the sudden, heavy high, his knees falling out from under him with only Pike's grip keeping him upright. The colours of the world changed from red to purple to blue to green to white to —

Too many colours, colours he'd never seen before, and he was sinking, his own skin singing with painful ecstasy, beneath their depths.

* * *

Gellert knew when he woke up that he must have been out for hours, if not the whole day, and he shifted on the bed he was on top of, touching the fleece blanket that had been thrown over him. He was still dressed, except for his shoes — that was good.

"You taste great," said Pike, which was less so. "Might want to drink a bit more orange juice in the mornings, though."

Gellert's jaw was slow, wouldn't move, much like the rest of his body, and so he didn't say anything, didn't respond. He could feel a strange heaviness throughout all of his limbs, and the hangover from the venom was heavy and slow to dissipate.

A glass was brought up to his mouth, and for the second time in Pike's presence he opened his mouth and sucked down the straw given to him, taking in the water. It was a strangely laborious movement, hollowing his cheeks and swallowing, but Pike let him stay still for a little while, letting him come back to his senses.

"Change your mind?" asked Pike.

Every limb feeling weighted down with sand, Gellert felt on the bed for the edge, felt that he was on the left side, and Pike was to his left too, a shadow beside the mostly blacked-out windows, but with enough light coming in to show his silhouette.

"Can you *see*?" asked Pike, sounding abruptly interested, and Gellert looked directly at his silhouette, doing his best to give the illusion of his eyes focusing on his face.

"Of course," said Gellert.

"You little fucking liar," said Pike. "Don't you wear glasses?"

"Ask your big helper," muttered Gellert. "He's the one who stood on them while he was kidnapping me."

"Shit," said Pike. "You really can't see me?"

"Let me go."

"As if you can walk."

"Let me go when I can."

"Have I said I wouldn't?"

No aspirate "h" sound — *'ave* I, he said; a buzzing sound on some of the sibilant "s"s, not as soft as they might be in someone else's mouth; his "l"s more like "w"s, *reawy* can't see me; the d of *wouldn't* swallowed, so that the word became monosyllabic...

Gellert had hated his speech therapist as a child. Funny how much his idle chatter about accent and dialect filtered back to him in times like this, the better to soothe his anxiety.

Perhaps he'd write and tell him, were the man not already dead, and had Gellert not already danced on his grave.

Gellert didn't try to stand as Pike got up, trying to focus on actually feeling his legs before he relied on them to support his weight, and when Pike returned a few minutes later he rifled through something on the bed beside him. Gellert tried to reach for it, blindly grasping for it, but Pike moved it further down the bed.

"My briefcase?" asked Gellert.

"You can see it?"

"I can smell the leather," he said. "Hear it creak."

"You got a keen nose, keen set of ears on you, too. Almost as keen as mine."

"I'm afraid I can't sense anyone's heartbeat at a hundred paces." He hesitated, and then asked, "Are you going to kill me?"

"Not planning to just yet," said Pike, and gently slid Gellert's spare glasses on. He was very delicate about them, holding the frames carefully in his big hands and pushing them up his nose, sliding them into place.

He wouldn't have recognised Pike even if he had been wearing them — Pike was far bigger than he expected, but squarer too. He had a cleft in his broad chin and a wide jaw, and his hair was shaved on one side and long on the other, a piece of gold jewellery wrapped around his ear's shell.

The ear — both of them, presumably — was small and pointed, and Gellert realised he'd never really imagined that in his mental image of what Lucien Pike actually looked like, even though his ears were almost always the first thing people mentioned.

Pike had pale brown skin and long, birch-bark coloured hair. His skin had purple undertones, but it was a subtle colouring, and his eyes were unusually large and reddish brown in colour.

It was plain to look at him that he had fae blood, the colour palette not quite right to be a human, and Gellert's eyes dropped to the second thing people often mentioned when describing him: his fangs, which were permanently retracted, protruded slightly from his upper gums and dug slightly into his lower lips.

He was devastatingly attractive, but then, Gellert had been warned of that before.

"You know why I lost my job," said Gellert. "You really think I want to go from one criminal's den to another?"

"Criminal?" asked Pike, wounded, spreading a hand on his chest. He had neatly buffed, short fingernails with blunt edges, but the many rings he was wearing looked sharp. "Me?"

"Everyone's a criminal in Lashton," said Gellert.

"That includes you, don't it?" asked Pike, and Gellert looked up at him, at the confidence painted on his features like it belonged there. "You tried to stab me. All I've done is give you a little bite. You bent your knife, by the away."

He dropped the blade into Gellert's lap, and Gellert picked it up, stroking his thumb over the blade — the graze it had given him was only a little sore, and he hadn't drawn blood. Where the knife was bent on its hinge, it wouldn't fold back.

"Bend it back," he said, "and I'll hear you out."

Pike said, "Deal," and took it. He had very big thighs, Gellert could see, stuffed into tight, pin-striped trousers, and he wasn't wearing a collared shirt under the matching blazer, but an equally tight, v-neck shirt. Pike leaned back in his seat and put his feet on the bed beside Gellert's hip, crossing his ankles over one another. He bent the knife back in one, impossibly easy movement of very strong hands. "Word has it people want you dead, after all that business yesterday."

"It's really not special that people want me dead," said Gellert, taking his knife back and folding the blade back in. "You're familiar with the sensation yourself, I take it."

"You grow up here?" asked Pike. "In Lashton?"

"Yes."

"How old are you?"

"Thirty-one."

"Thirty years without pissing anyone off, and suddenly you start making enemies," said Pike mildly. *Firty* years, *wivout, pissin, makin.* Gellert catalogued every inflection like he was cupping running water between his hands, capturing it mid-flow. He liked the differences in people's accents — he didn't hear many London accents in Lashton, but he liked to hear them.

He liked Pike's voice, liked the slight hoarseness, the throatiness to it, the strength of his accent and his pronunciation, liked how deep in tone it was. He liked how his mouth moved as he pronounced each word.

"I don't care for being threatened, nor insulted," said Gellert.

"What happened?"

"You don't know?"

"Not the specifics," said Pike, shrugging his great shoulders, He leaned forward to slide off his suit jacket, and Gellert looked at his shirt, the way it was tight around his huge chest, the curve of his belly, the way his mighty shoulders were almost bursting out of the sleeves. "I know the Laithes want you blotted out, and the Kings too — yesterday you was everybody's friend."

"No, I wasn't," said Gellert.

"Heh. No, you wasn't. In fact, most people din't know your name — but that's right, for someone like you. Now people *do* know your name, it's 'cause they want you dead."

"Into every life a drop of rain must fall."

"You don't like people, do ya?" asked Pike.

Gellert frowned slightly, glancing at Pike's face. "What gives you that idea?" he asked.

"Well, you come off like a cunt," said Pike.

"You kidnapped me. For all you know, I'm as sweet as a debutante with most acquaintances."

"You isn't," said Pike.

"No, I'm not, but that's hardly the point."

Pike crossed two big, heavy arms over his big, heavy chest, and when he leaned back in his seat, it creaked underneath him. Even with his legs crossed, Gellert could see the sizable bulge in his trousers — that was the third thing people mentioned about Lucien Pike, if it wasn't the first.

"You grew up in Lashton," said Pike. "You know how to handle yourself, don'tcha? Word is people don't like you."

"Oh no," said Gellert sarcastically. "That hurts my feelings."

"'Cause you're on the spectrum."

"Colour spectrum?"

"Asperger's."

"Asperger's," Gellert repeated, and scoffed. "Even when they diagnosed me, I wasn't palatable enough to be labelled with Asperger's. I'm autistic."

"And blind as shit," said Pike. "And you talk funny. And you're a cunt."

"And you want to hire me," said Gellert.

Pike grinned, showing his sharp fangs. "Yeah," he said.

"Now who's the cunt between us?"

"What's the different between Asperger's and autistic?"

"Politics, acceptability, and about fifteen years."

"You're a savant, though."

"Why, because I can do a few sums without hunching over a calculator?"

"You're fucking violent," said Pike thoughtfully, looking mildly impressed. "Din't know people like you could be good with knives."

"Not that good, evidently," said Gellert.

"Well, there's no point stabbing me," said Pike. "But you speared Dandy pretty fucking good, word is."

"Well, what else was I supposed to do?"

"Do you think people hate you more 'cause you're a faggot, or 'cause of the autism?"

"Always asking the important questions, aren't you?"

"Is it true you're a trap?" asked Pike, and Gellert blinked.

"I beg your pardon?"

"You know, a cuntboy," said Pike. "You had your womb whipped out and your tits chopped off, but you still have an axe wound."

"Oh," said Gellert, filing "trap" away to remember for later, and doing his best to do anything *but* remember "axe wound". "The politically correct term is transgender, but yes."

"You're not getting angry," said Pike.

"Are you trying to make me angry?"

"Not really," said Pike. "Just wanted to see if you would be. You too good for crime?"

"Stealing doesn't bother me, least of all from the king," Gellert muttered, experimentally shifting his legs, his arms, which still felt numb with mindless pleasure from Pike's venom. "And I don't care about the fae trading unions."

"What, you're just stupid?"

"The wholesaler belongs to the Kings, as well you know. Dai Laithe comes in, demands I hold a package for him. I didn't want to."

"How come?"

"I didn't care for his tone."

Pike was smiling at him, lips curled up into it, teeth imprinting into his lower lip. "You proud little bitch."

"Dai tried to lean on my cashier, who's already an anxious soul, and when I came to intervene, he whirled on me. I don't much care for being called a speccy little cunt by a teenager trying to throw his weight around, so I threw him out. Physically. Hardly my fault he tripped on the cobbles and fell in the mud in front of a group of Renns and Sorrels."

Pike laughed, clapping his great hands together. "Yeah," he said delightedly. "I seen the pics going around, I din't realise it was from that."

A centuries-old vampire saying "pics" annoyed him, somehow, but Gellert didn't give voice to that.

"So the Laithes want me dead for humiliating one of their youngest — not, in their eyes, a proportionate response to a rude demand."

"Prob'ly in't proportional," said Pike. "He's only a stupid kid."

"I'd had a hard day," said Gellert. "Stressful. I lost my temper where I oughtn't — and in the process, lost rather a lot else, besides."

Pike watched him for a few moments, and then asked, "What about the Kings?"

"Dandy wanted to humiliate me in turn," said Gellert. "Smooth hurt feelings. He had tar or something, enchanted — I've seen the tar and feather routine before, and I wasn't about to submit myself to it. I stabbed him in the shoulder when he came at me in lieu of my week's notice."

"You're a *very* proud bitch," said Pike admiringly, and then added, "I won't humiliate you."

"You'll just interrogate every potentially sensitive aspect of my identity and drink from me when you please?"

"Wanted to see what you tasted like," said Pike, as though it were, in some way, normal or acceptable. "I don't hire people I don't like the taste of. Thought it'd be easier to bite you than get you to spread your legs."

Gellert, skin hot, made the decision not to respond to that.

"I'm *not* a secretary," said Gellert. "I have my Bachelor's in Mathematics and Accounting. I've managed that business and both books for nearly eight years — I can handle the cops, I can handle interfamilial disputes, and for all my numerous personal defects, I am a *good* manager."

"Exactly," said Pike. "You know how to file things and keep appointments and be organised and that, and manage a whole business. That's what I want — and no one would dare kill my secretary."

Gellert was quiet for a few moments, very still. People complained sometimes, about how still he got when he was thinking — Dandy often commented on it, when they were working in the office alongside one another, how unnatural his stillness was, but he was only still after a great deal of training.

It used to be his movements that people found unnatural. The thing people truly found unnatural was Gellert himself, it seemed to him, regardless of how he presented himself.

"Why me?" he asked. "You must admit that snapping up a man just because someone else is about to have him killed is not a normal hiring process."

"An't found the right person, yet," said Pike. "Used to be I din't need one, but the business is expanding now, and I need it organised."

"They keep leaving you, you mean, and you want someone who can't get tired of your shit and walk out."

"They don't all leave me for my personality," said Pike, and grinned. "I got the last two pregnant."

Gellert shifted his knees together under the blanket. "Well," he said quietly, "that won't be a problem with me."

"I know," said Pike. "*Very* handy."

"Because I won't let you fuck me, I mean," snapped Gellert.

Pike shrugged, undeterred. "They all say that."

"I don't want to be a fucking secretary," said Gellert. "Least of all yours."

"Well, no one else is gonna hire you, and trust me when I say you won't make it outta town alive," said Pike, leering. "You smell good, taste good. You don't wanna work in my office, I can hire you to work somewhere else in the house."

His implication was less than subtle.

"This isn't a house," said Gellert.

Pike frowned. "Huh?"

"We're at the old hospital on Carrot Hill," said Gellert. "It took me a while — you've obviously had some of the rooms refurbished, these bedrooms, the office, and we came the back way through the conservatory, but I counted the turns from outside the florist where your men picked me up."

"Fuck," said Pike, frowning at him and idly scratching his fingers through the thick stubble on his cheeks. "In't you a sharp little fucking needle? Well, now *I* have to kill you, if you won't take the job."

"I'll take it," muttered Gellert. "I'll take your fucking job."

"Good," said Pike. "In my office, or the other thing?"

"Are you even gay?"

"Any hole's a goal, mate. But I do like — do you mind if I call it a cunt?"

"I prefer cunt to axe wound. What else would I want you to call it?"

"Uh, front hole? Gender neutral, innit?"

"Jesus H. Christ," said Gellert.

One of Pike's feet, clad in a thick sock, slid against Gellert's thigh: even through the wool and Gellert's trousers, his foot was very cold.

"I'll do your paperwork and your appointments. Keep your cock in your trousers."

"What if it don't fit?"

"You fixed my knife — I can fix that for you in turn."

Pike laughed, shaking his head. "Fucking lethal, you is. I hear you killed a man in '06."

"I didn't."

"Nah?"

"I was involved in the lead-up to his death."

"He tripped out a window after talking with you. He was built like a brick fucking shitter, and a man like that don't just tip over."

"People trip, and have nasty accidents," said Gellert blankly, "and it's very tragic."

"Did he trip, or did you push him?" asked Pike.

Gellert inhaled through his nostrils, but that was the only outward reaction he allowed himself. "May I have another glass of water?"

"Yeah, 'course," said Pike. "Or squash — you want squash? Lemonade?"

"Orange squash."

"Right." He didn't get up, but sent a text on a huge brick of a phone that looked miniscule between Gellert's huge fingers.

"'Course," said Pike, "if it was you killed him, they wouldn't ever say. He was an MMA champ and he won duels and shit, Gwyn Fickle. He was near seven feet — less embarrassing for him to die in an accident than be killed by some spotty sixteen-year-old."

"You have my whole life story laid out, don't you? One wonders what the need was for all those questions."

"Had to do my research," said Pike. "Din't have your CV."

"Fucking ask next time," said Gellert. "You've shown yourself more than capable of posing questions."

"I like my way better, makes it easier to see if you're lying. Could fuck you now, if you like."

"You drugged me up, could have fucked me then."

Pike bristled, looking appalled. "The fuck d'you take me for?" he demanded.

Gellert arched his eyebrow, tapping his knife against his palm before flicking it open and then shut again — Pike had been more than strong enough to bend it perfectly straight, so that now it moved as smoothly as it ever had.

"How many people have you killed this year?" Gellert asked. "Not your crew — just you, personally."

"That's different," said Pike.

"And all those people you've impregnated?"

"They all consented," said Pike. "*Enthusiastically.*" Consen'ed. Enfusiastic'ly. "I got a big dick, and I know how to use it. Know how to use my tongue and my fingers and all."

"But not how to use a condom."

Pike scoffed. "Defeats the point of fucking someone, wearing a condom. If I wanted to stick my dick in a bit of latex I'd get a toy."

"So you're riddled with STIs."

"Vampiric-fae immune system," said Pike smugly. "Beats everything else into submission."

"I'm not letting you fuck me."

"Not yet."

Gellert sighed. "I'll look at your office," he said. "See where to start."

"I could go down on you," Pike suggested.

The door opened, and a woman in a suit brought in a tray of pastries with two glasses of squash, setting it down on the edge of the bed beside Gellert. She handed Pike a sheaf of papers, which he squinted at with evident distaste.

Her belly, Gellert noticed, was significantly protruding from under her maternity blouse, and she couldn't button her blazer if she wanted to — as Pike was looking at the paper, he grabbed at her arse with the other hand.

He got up to follow her out as Gellert picked up his drink. "Be right back," he said, unzipping the side of her skirt, and she laughed, pulling him after her.

Gellert looked in his bag for his phone, his hands still slow and lacking their normal dexterity, but not as bad as they had been.

No missed calls, no texts. He wasn't due to go to see his mother until tomorrow, so at least there was no cause for her to worry, not that she could really text him if she was.

He sighed, falling back against the pillows, and pulled the tray closer.

* * *

A few hours later, when he was able to actually walk around without stumbling, Gellert asked, "Am I just maternity cover then?" He was no longer working through the haze of lingering venom, but he still felt slow and clumsy.

"Huh? Nah, Christina is gonna go live with her parents in Cornwall."

"Right. You're not worried about your new offspring living so far away?"

"Why would I be? She's not gonna want to fuck when she has a baby hanging off her tit and keeping her up all night, and it'll take weeks for her to tighten up again."

A feminist, Pike was not.

Lucien Pike was a man known for his numerous bastards, and one could see the evidence of his sowing of wild oats throughout Lashton as a whole — a good few of his peers at school, in his own year or in the others, had had pointed ears or protruding teeth or strong faces like Pike's. Gellert's history teacher was a Pike, a lilac-skinned woman whose fangs were always down. It was a family trait, not being able to retract them.

Come to think of it, the vampire girl he'd experimented with as a child had had the same trait and red eyes, and Gellert tried not to think in too much detail about the implications of that.

He'd barely been able to see it earlier, but now with his glasses on he could see that Pike's office was a fucking mess, papers piled up on every other surface, a calendar on one wall with post-its in terrible handwriting all over it.

He opened a filing cabinet at random and winced.

"Did you pick *any* of your last assistants for their organisational skills?" he asked dryly. "Or even for their cleanliness?"

"Sure," said Pike, and Gellert turned to look at him critically. Pike deflated slightly. "At first. Some of 'em get intimidated by people in town, other families, or by the Bill."

Gellert sighed, and looked at his watch.

"Very well," he said. "Get out."

"'Scuse me?" asked Pike.

"I'm sure you understood me quite well. I need to start working on all this without you leering at me or distracting me with stupid questions. Off you go. I'm sure there's someone for you to shake down or stick your cock in or however you occupy your time."

Pike's mood, which had been resoundingly cheerful since first laying eyes on him, turned to one of distaste, and his red-brown eyes were very cold in feeling if not in colour.

"You don't fucking tell me what to do," he growled.

"I believe you told me this was equivalent to my management position."

"That don't mean you're fucking managing *me*."

"Alright," said Gellert. "Then I quit."

Pike shoved him back against one of the cabinets, glaring down at him with one big hand squeezing around Gellert's throat. Gellert distantly wondered if this was the sort of temper tantrum he was hoping to provoke out of Gellert with his litany of personal questions earlier on.

"Then I'll kill you," he hissed.

"And if you kill me," said Gellert, albeit chokingly, "your office stays the same."

Pike squeezed harder, and then let go.

Coughing, Gellert massaged his throat, and he looked up at Pike's face, at the deep scowl twisting his pale lilac lips.

"You want what your competitors have, I presume, the edge you know they have over you," said Gellert. "Neat, tidy books, neat, tidy accounts and offices, all headed by neat, tidy people. I'm your man, if that's what you want, but you *must* leave me to it."

"You're not the fucking boss here," growled Pike. "I could slit you open from mouth to cunt."

"I've no doubt of that," said Gellert coolly. "And then what, you'll try the agency again? Swing your equipment about in the nearest recruitment office and see who you draw in?"

Pike laughed at that, a low, grim sound.

"You got no sense of fucking self-preservation," said Pike.

"You knew that," Gellert pointed out. "Those are the conditions under which you hired me, and you did your research. You know I don't suffer fools, you know I don't hold my tongue. You have not employed my services because you want me to hold your hand or be your bestest pal — you want me to fix your office, which is, as it stands, a fucking pigsty. Either allow me to attend to these duties, or kill me, but this faffing about is embarrassing for both of us."

Pike looked down at him critically for a long few moments. Then, with great deliberation, he asked, "You good at sucking cock?"

Gellert rolled his eyes. "Get out, Pike."

"*Mr* Pike," the vampire corrected. "I'm your boss, in't I?"

"Please, Mr Pike," Gellert simpered venomously, "if sir would be so good as to allow me to my work."

"*Sir*," said Pike, and laughed as he went. "No one's called me that in half a century."

"You don't say," muttered Gellert.

He shut the door behind Pike's retreating form.

* * *

At some time past noon, Yves lumbered into the room with a tray of sandwiches and set it down on a clear part of Pike's desk. Gellert was mostly organising papers on the floor, to ensure he had the space for everything; two bin bags had already been filled with a mix of nonsense and literal, actual rubbish from the cabinets.

"Thank you," said Gellert crisply. "Is your wrist healing alright?"

Yves rubbed his bandaged forearm. "They made me have six stitches and a tetanus shot," he said sourly. "They thought it was a dog, chunk you took out of me."

"Well, you work with a vampire," Gellert replied. "I'm sure bites in the course of the duty are de rigeur."

Yves grumbled under his breath as he left Gellert to it, and he was permitted his peace until past six. Pike lingered in the doorway to peer in, hesitating before he crossed the threshold.

"Oh," he said, stepping inside. "Yves said you had paper everywhere."

"I did," Gellert said. "Until I washed the crumbs, blood, syrup, and what I'm choosing not to believe was semen from out of your filing cabinets and dried the mess. Now, everything is neatly away in order for me to digitise later."

"Digitise?" repeated Pike — digi'ise.

Gellert didn't need it to keep himself calm anymore: he just liked the rhythm of Pike's voice.

"Put it all on a computer."

"Don't 'ave a computer."

"Well, it will be a nice change for you, won't it?"

Pike hummed, and curiously opened a cabinet, apparently fascinated by the neatly compartmentalised result of Gellert's labour within.

"D'you want to go home?" he asked.

"Firing me already?"

"Oh, no," said Pike, turning to glance at him. "I meant, you scared to go home? D'you want to stay here?"

"Oh," said Gellert. "No, I'm not frightened in the least. I'll be here tomorrow morning, bright and early — we must discuss remuneration."

"Twenty an hour?"

"Discussion complete."

"You don't wanna haggle? I might go higher."

"No, twenty will serve me just fine for now. I'll be here tomorrow at eight."

"... That early? Again? How about twelve?"

"I'll be here at eight," said Gellert crisply. "Leave a card or cash for me to get you a computer, and we can discuss it when you wake. In the evening, after work, I'll go to visit my mother. I do that thrice a week, I will expect it to be accommodated."

"'Course," said Pike immediately. "Ten?"

"Eight."

Pike sighed. "One of the boys will drive you home."

Perhaps unsurprisingly, it wasn't Yves that volunteered for this, but one of the smaller men that had assisted in his kidnapping before — a son or other relative of Pike's, Gellert suspected, because he saw the similarities in the shape of his nose, his forehead, the point of his ears and sharp teeth.

Siân and Dag Laithe were waiting outside his flat when Gellert arrived home. When Dag put his hand on Gellert's shoulder, Gellert shifted hard to bend his fingers back, and they cracked very loudly; as Siân came at him from the other side, Gellert announced, "I've found new employment."

He dodged her grasping hand as she started to snap, "Who gives a
—"

"I'm Lucien Pike's new assistant." He said it cleanly. It wasn't
intended to make her stop, only to stumble, but she froze for a second
to stare at him, and he walked between her and Dag cradling his fingers,
closing his flat door behind him and locking it, too.

"That doesn't mean you're safe!" she called belatedly through the
door.

"I think you'll find it does!" he called back, rifling through his post,
and he put the poison letter — a King tradition, when acknowledging
one's severance — aside to be burned.

Dag and Siân argued in hushed voices before they went off.

BOBBY SEYS YOUR HOME ALRITE, buzzed his phone.
WANT ME TO KILL THEM??

"Do you have to text in all caps?" he retorted, and then undressed to
shower.

He slept that night surprisingly well.

* * *

"It's on my desk," said Pike distastefully when he came into his office just
before one. He was visibly somewhat sleepy, his hair messy and mussed
with the morning.

"Yes," agreed Gellert. "That's where a computer goes. It will take me
time to digitise your books — do you know already who's skimming off
the top?"

"Mm, should be a few, I can give you the names. Why, numbers seem
off?"

"Books make it harder to compare side by side," Gellert murmured.
"Especially over time, and you may have unexpected embezzlers. Once I
have everything on a spreadsheet, it'll become a lot tougher to obfuscate
— though not impossible. Have you any meetings?"

"Mm," grunted Pike.

"... Yes," said Gellert. "When?"

Pike shrugged.

"With whom?"

"Uh, other bosses. Suppliers. Officers. You know."

Gellert pressed his lips together, and exhaled through his nostrils. "Nothing urgent, at least?"

"Maybe, I dunno. I need you today."

"Me?"

"Yeah."

"To watch you threaten people?"

"Want minutes," said Pike.

He looked tired.

"Fine," said Gellert, and kept working.

The meeting was with Dag Laithe, whose hand was in a cast. He started crying within minutes, before Pike had even done much to him.

The Laithes didn't bother him again, after that.

"Kings send you one of them venom letters?" Pike asked afterward.

"Yes."

"Want me to do something to them?"

"Hm, to protect my honour?"

Pike frowned, brow furrowing. "Protect my secretary," he said. "Self-defence, innit?"

"Oh, how quaint. No, Mr Pike, I don't think so — it was tradition, not anything personal. You can hardly go around taking offence to tradition in Lashton. You'll be taking offence to everything."

"Mmm," Pike rumbled. "Want a shag?"

"I'll survive without."

"What's wrong with your mum?"

Gellert blinked, and turned to look at Pike in the car, not quite certain how to respond to that less than smooth segue. Pike looked back at him, unflinching.

"She has a degenerative nerve disease called ALS. Amytrophic lateral sclerosis. It's defined primarily by an increasing loss of motor function — as the disease progressives, the muscles become stiff or prone to spasms, and then they begin to waste away. My mother was diagnosed about seven years ago, and has been in the hospice for four. She can't do very much on her own anymore — can't walk even with crutches, gets tired speaking too much, even. As time goes on, she'll have difficulty chewing, swallowing, and then she'll have difficulty breathing on her own.

"Her cognitive function is not tremendously impaired most days — she still understands conversation even on the days she can't participate, still likes to listen to audiobooks and watch films, enjoys when I complain about work or tell her about politics in the city. On the days when her brain is too foggy, she just likes quiet company, a little music."

"I'd wanna be put down if that was me," said Pike.

"Alright," said Gellert. "I'll note that down for future reference."

"Does it hurt?"

"Yes," said Gellert. "I don't believe it's agony, but it's severe discomfort when it isn't pain. Much of her difficulty thinking, on days when thinking is hard, is caused by that, I think. But she's been very lucky."

"How the fuck is that lucky?"

"She's lived longer than most people do," said Gellert. "She has someone who loves her and visits her, is attended to in a well-staffed hospice, has access to robust analgesics. She will die, but we all will."

"Why don't you put her out of her misery?" asked Pike, and Gellert wondered if it was another attempt to provoke him, or if it was just that Pike was really, truly this blunt and tactless. Every conversation with him was like a personal interrogation, and Gellert didn't know if he was mad for finding his bluntness refreshing.

"I asked her if she wanted me to," said Gellert. "She said she didn't. At such a point as her circumstances change, I have no doubt she'll let me know."

"She can't always talk, you said."

"She can communicate what she needs to," said Gellert. "She's my mother — I respect her wishes, and purely selfishly, I enjoy going to see her every few days. I'll miss her, when she's dead."

"S'that gonna happen to you?" asked Pike. "The ALS?"

"No, I don't think so, the doctors didn't think it was familial," said Gellert. "But there's no guarantee. I won't know for a few more years."

"Don't it scare you?" asked Pike.

"I suppose," said Gellert.

"You was her nurse at home," said Pike. "'Fore she went into hospital."

"Yes. I had some training — I'm hardly a qualified nurse, but I could care for her, until her symptoms worsened and she needed more round the clock care. But you knew that — you asked around, I expect, and I'm sure you know I inject my own testosterone."

Pike nodded, his hands over his belly.

"I have three people in shift in the hospital," he said after letting a few beats pass. "Soon as we picked you up, and I knew the Kings wanted you dead. You can introduce 'em to her, if you want, they can help change her audiobooks or read her shit, since they'll be there anyways." He hesitated, frowning. "I think they can all read. You'll have to double check."

Gellert looked at Pike's face, at the neutral expression there. He looked generally affable, didn't seem at all proud of himself, or even as though he'd done anything particularly remarkable, watching Lashton pass by outside the car's window.

"You put guards on my mother," said Gellert slowly, "before I even took the job?"

"Well, be shit if one of 'em killed her, wouldn't it?" asked Pike. "If she don't want to be dead, and you don't want her dead neither. I don't like shit like that, think it's underhanded."

"How noble of you."

Pike grinned. "Yeah," he said.

Gellert repressed the urge to roll his eyes, and hid his reluctant smile behind his hand.

* * *

What Gellert hadn't taken into account — and he should have — was that people in Lashton might try to threaten him for his employer's sins rather than his own. It made sense, of course: for all his association with Pike might shield him for the consequences of his own misdeeds, Pike offended far *more* people than Gellert ever had, and Gellert was far more accessible than his new employer, if someone wanted to send a message.

The reality of this set in when, on his day off, he found himself standing in his bathroom over the corpse of a man he'd never seen before. He took him by the hair, pulling his head back — the body was fresh, and not yet stiff — to send a photo of his face to Yves, because Pike's brick couldn't manage emojis, let alone JPGs.

Pike called him less than a minute later, and Gellert didn't really listen as he loudly worked his way through various threats and invocations, pushing the corpse further back into his bath so that it didn't drip on his bathmat.

It was best to let Pike work through his temper before expecting him to think.

"It's 'cause we're expanding," said Pike once he'd calmed down. "More product coming down from Alba, and from the Bretons too, and I have that new factory here in the hospital. We have the mushrooms growing down in the basement, and production is proper fast."

"And who is this man?"

"Well, he *was* one of my distributors in London, was spreading word about new supply. But I guess dropping him on you is a threat."

"Yes, I'm sure they'd like to upset me in the hopes I throw you off your balance, I do follow. Would someone come pick this corpse up?"

"Yeah, I'll use it."

"... I meant to dispose of it," said Gellert, "and perhaps alert his family, but alright. I should expect more of this?"

"Prob'ly."

"Right, well, I'll see you tomorrow, I need to get dressed."

Pike perked up audibly. "You naked?"

"I'm just out of the shower — I think the corpse was already in the bath, though, I was in a stupor before I was under the spray."

"You wet?"

"No, I'm towelled off for the most part."

Pike grumbled, "No, I meant your —"

Gellert hung up.

Yves collected the corpse, wrapped him neatly in a piece of tarpaulin, and was very careful not to drip any blood or assorted goo onto Gellert's floors, which Gellert appreciated immensely.

He *liked* Yves, and much of Yves' bad will toward Gellert for biting his arm open dissipated when Gellert offered to take the stitches out for him and re-dress the wound himself, so he didn't have to go back to the hospital.

"You've been working for Mr Pike a long time?" Gellert asked as he worked, and Yves didn't look away as Gellert carefully and neatly pulled out each stitch, only mildly wincing at the occasional tug of not-quite-pain as the skin moved.

"Yeah," said Yves. "I started ferrying stuff when I was nine, and I got noticed 'cause I was good at it, never got caught even when I was moving bigger stuff. Wanted to make it so my mum didn't have to work, 'cause my dad was in a wheelchair and he couldn't work any longer, and I'm the oldest of four. That was years ago, though — they live in a nice house out in Llallwg now. Mr Pike pays good."

"How old are you?" asked Gellert curiously.

"Forty-three."

"You don't look it," said Gellert. "You look younger than I do."

"Black don't crack," said Yves. "And I think you know you look pretty shit for your age, even as far as malnourished white boys go."

Gellert laughed and gave a small nod of his head. "No pain?" he checked in.

"Nah," said Yves. "Thanks for this. I don't like hospitals anyway, and there's always cops hanging around."

"Well, it's rather the least I can do, being as I'm the architect of these new scars of yours. Going to tell people it was a dog?"

"Nah," said Yves. "You're gonna have a reputation soon enough — you're already getting one, and I bet it'll be a good story to have Gellert Osgodby's teeth ripped into my arm in two years' time. You aren't a fucking background middle manager anymore. People take notice of someone like you, once you've got a name."

"My name was Dandy King's, once," said Gellert in measured tones. "I don't see why things should be different when my name is Lucien Pike's."

"You know he does things different," said Yves. "And anyway, that was one thing when you were up in an office out of the way, but you're his left hand now, if not his right. People take notice of that kinda shit — they do for me."

"All I do is take minutes," said Gellert, and trimmed out the last of the stitches, pulling his kit bag closer to run antiseptic over the almost-healed wounds, which were all nice and clean.

"Yeah," said Yves. "You keep telling yourself that."

When he went back into Pike's office, Pike was leaning back in his chair and talking on loudspeaker with a supplier in a thick language Gellert had no hope of understanding — it was either Breton or Cornish, he thought, but it could just as easily be Manx or some other Celtic language he'd not had much exposure to, but would no doubt come to learn.

Pike's hand came to rest on the curve of Gellert's arse, and Gellert absentmindedly slapped his hand away as he took up Pike's coffee mug, taking it to pour a refill for both Pike and himself.

He had become used to Pike's wandering hands, in the past few weeks — most of the time, Pike pretended to be correcting some article of Gellert's clothing, but Gellert's waistband had never needed correcting before in his life, and the pretence was a shallow one; sometimes, Pike just rested his hand on Gellert's waist or his arse, rarely on his knee or thigh, but he didn't tend to squeeze.

It was, at most, mildly irritating, and yet somehow, Pike's leering, frequent invitations for sex, and tendency to actually touch Gellert somehow didn't measure up to Dandy King's own occasional movements in that direction.

They'd never fucked, he and Dandy — Dandy hadn't been interested until a few years ago, when Gellert had had an ongoing, purely sexual arrangement with Courageous King, and the two of them regularly met up to fuck.

It had bothered Dandy at the time — he'd thought Gellert was looking for promotion within the family, particularly given that Courageous was so much higher ranking than his brother, and was entrusted with far more command, and a territorial nature had given way to a fetishistic curiosity about Gellert's cunt, about what it felt like, what Gellert's body was like. Gellert vaguely recalled Dandy shutting down his phone very quickly several times, each time showing some twink with a well-used cunt on the screen, and occasionally he would ask pointed questions, ask if Gellert had a boyfriend.

His interest had fizzled out somewhat after Gellert had taken up with a local bike mechanic instead, one that Dandy didn't know, and had fizzled even further after his hysterectomy, but it had never faded entirely.

There was something different about Pike's objectification of him — perhaps it was refreshing simply because he was so blunt and obvious about it, made no attempt to hide it, and because he objectified almost every person he saw.

He did, for the most part, keep his hands to himself outside of his own employees: Gellert had noticed that even in bars and restaurants, Pike didn't reach out to touch wait staff or dancers unless they touched him first, and it was only the ones who knew him as a regular that invited that, often sitting in his lap or leaning over his shoulder.

The same did not apply to other smugglers — Pike well knew how to use his size and his sexuality to intimidate, and Gellert watched him do it not irregularly.

It was three months into Gellert's employment with Pike that after a business lunch, where Gellert had been taking minutes in a coded shorthand to type up later, that some of the Laithes came into the same restaurant. It was neutral ground, had been for a century, but that hardly precluded a clash from time to time.

Their table was a large-set booth with wide benches and a good deal of space, so that despite the fact that Yves and the two largest of the pixie dust distributors were each of them over six feet tall and broad, they were able to sit down comfortably. Pike didn't care to be hemmed in by the booth, though, and he sat at a large chair with arms they'd brought over for him, sitting at the head of the table.

Gellert was sitting at the very edge of the booth, at Pike's left side, with Yves on the other side of him — Pike had made fun of Gellert for wanting to be able to see the door, but he hadn't actually made him move further in.

The Laithes didn't see this right away — or at least, young Dai Laithe didn't, because he saw Gellert, idly picking at crisps from his plate, and rushed over, striding with his shoulders back and his head high.

He skidded to a stop in front of Gellert, and very abruptly seemed to realise that Gellert was not, in fact, alone, the rest of the table no longer obscured by the walls of the booth or the pub's support pillars.

It was rather like watching a ship's full sails torn as they billowed: he stopped so suddenly that he teetered, and his wide eyes went from the unimpressed Gellert to the eight men he was sitting with, especially Lucien Pike himself, widening further.

Dag, his hand now healed and out of its splint, and Siân, looking furious, were chasing swiftly after their younger brother, but it was plain that they didn't want to run as eagerly as Dai had, because others in the restaurant were looking.

"Hello, Mr Laithe," said Gellert, after a moment of watching Dai's mouth open and close, sheer terror rendering him silent. Gellert took pity on him, and stood to his feet. "My apologies, Mr Pike, I'll —"

"This the Laithes' youngest?" asked Pike, turning to look at Dai. "Dafydd?"

"Sorry," said Dai. "Thought I saw someone I knew, I'll just —"

"*Ah*," said Pike, and grabbed Dai by one of the fashionable belt loops of his skinny trousers, and Gellert didn't allow his face to show even a hint of reaction as Pike hauled Dai into his lap. Dai was dragged to sit on the heavy pillow of Pike's hard thighs, and already, he was pink and shaking. "No, I'm sure he had something to say," said Pike, and one of his big hands wrapped demonstratively around Dai's waist, the other curling around his upper thigh, keeping him in place as though he were a marionette. "Didn't you, lad?"

Dai Laithe looked so terrified he seemed almost frightened to breathe, but Gellert could see the way he flinched when Pike's huge hand squeezed the meat of his thigh.

"Wanted to introduce yourself to another family's boss," said Pike. "Show you're on the map, s'that it?"

Laithe's lips quivered, but they didn't move, and Gellert's own hands clenched at his sides into tight fists.

The others in Pike's retinue, bar Yves, were trying not to laugh, all of them watching the way Pike moved his knee under Dai's arse and tipped him slightly forward, and as Gellert watched, still, his fingers were sliding under the fabric of Dai Laithe's tight shirt, cool fingers touching the bare skin of his side and his belly.

It made Dai *squeak*, jumping in his seat, and that prompted a proper laugh from the other Pikes, but it was plain that Dai was too frightened and too nervous to shove Pike's hands off him.

"You shy?" asked Pike, breathing against the side of Dai's neck. Gellert felt nauseated. "You want me to do something to you you're too scared to ask for?"

Dai's eyes were watering as Pike's hand slid further up under his shirt, toward his chest, and Gellert could see Dag and Siân a foot off, not wanting to walk directly forward — this was between Dai and Pike, a personal dispute, no matter that it was between one boss and one most junior member of a far less powerful family, and if they intervened...

Well, at best, they'd humiliate their little brother even further — at worst, they were likely worried about provoking Pike into sparking a full conflict off the back of it.

"I think that's enough, Mr Pike, you've made your point," said Gellert in an undertone, leaning forward under the pretence of pushing Pike's plate back.

"He was coming to pick a fight with you, Gellert," said Pike, squeezing so high on Dai's thigh now that his thumb was pressed up against Dai's crotch, and Dai Laithe was shaking so hard he looked about ready to vibrate into another dimension, tears on his cheeks, his jaw set. "You know what they say. Make love, not war. If he tells me to let him go, I'll let him go."

Pike looked demonstratively at Dai, who let out a sob now, and Gellert, disgusted and furious, leaned directly over Dai's body, his hand on the other arm so that he could lean to look into Pike's eyes.

"Let him go right now," hissed Gellert, forcing himself to meet Pike's red gaze, no matter how unnatural it felt this close up. "You're embarrassing yourself."

"He fucking embarrassed *you* —"

"He's seventeen, he's a fucking idiot, and he didn't deserve what I did to him in the first place," Gellert snapped, keeping his voice quiet so that none of the others could hear him bar Yves, who looked almost as disapproving as Gellert did. "I expect you recall telling me I acted disproportionately, and I am doing you the same favour now. Feeling him up like this when he's crying, you're coming off like a right fucking nonce."

"He's legal, in't he? And he an't said no," retorted Pike. "And if he's too much of a prissy little quim to take *me* on, he shouldn't've come at you."

"Well, I think he's learned his lesson without you fucking fingering him for a crowd," said Gellert, and dragged Dai Laithe bodily out of Pike's lap.

Dai's knees were so weak with terror that he almost fell, and Gellert kept him up, not letting him hit the floor. Keeping a tight grip on the back of Dai's jacket collar, he took hold of the hem of the jacket on each side, straightening it out again before smoothing out his shirt front.

He barely touched Dai, careful to keep his touches on his clothes as he kept him upright, the better to keep him from actually hitting the floor.

After a few seconds, it was plain he wasn't collecting himself right away, and Gellert kept him upright and puppeted him forward until he was right in front of Dag and Siân.

"Take him," said Gellert through gritted teeth, his expression remaining neutral as a few people glanced their way, "or he'll fall."

Dag pretended to throw his arm around his brother, subtly hooking his hand under the bottom of his armpit to keep Dai from falling, and Gellert turned back to sit down at the table again.

Pike was simmering with undisguised rage at having his toy taken away.

"Mr Ramsay," said Gellert, slightly more loudly than he needed to, and with a pleasant smile. "Please, won't you let me know your assistant's number, and I'll forward her my minutes?"

* * *

"What the fuck was that?" Pike demanded as they came into Pike's office, and Gellert set his notebook beside Pike's computer on the desk, leaning his hands on the desk's surface to look at Pike properly.

"I might ask you the same question," Gellert retorted.

"He was coming to have a go," said Pike. "Couldn't you fucking see that? He was running so fast, stopped all of a sudden as soon as he saw —"

"*Yes*, of course I saw that," Gellert snapped, and Pike's lips drew back in a snarl, furious that he was being interrupted. "Couldn't you see he was already humiliated by that alone? That he'd shown himself overeager, that he'd bitten off more than he could chew? Posturing like that over a fucking child —"

"He's not a child!" Pike growled, moving forward like some great-shouldered, predatory cat, and Gellert automatically stepped back and away as Pike towered over him. "Seventeen years old — *that's* a man. When I was his age —"

"When you were his age, no one had invented indoor plumbing," Gellert spat, and Pike lunged at him.

Gellert's shoulders hit the plushly papered wall before his head did, his head tipping back against it after as Pike's hand wrapped tight around his throat, although he didn't squeeze, didn't stop Gellert from actually speaking, just pinned up against the wall on his tiptoes and kept him there.

"You undermined me," Pike growled.

"Undermined you?" Gellert repeated, and laughed bitterly. "I stopped you from humiliating yourself even more than you already were — what do you think it says to them, that you put all that effort into stringing out a teenager who's not done anything wrong — who did the smallest of things, in fact, which he has already been punished for? You come off as feral, as unmeasured, as big and fucking brutish as I know you are *not*. All because you insist on thinking with your fucking cock —"

"I wan't thinking with my cock!" Pike all but roared, so furious that there was spit flecking his sharp teeth in white bubbles of froth, and the sound made Gellert's head ache, made his ears pop, but he didn't try to pull away. "You think I want to fuck that skinny little prick? S'that what this is about, you're fucking jealous? I was showing I *could* —"

"Oh, of course you could, Mr Pike, anyone could! Anyone can glance at him and see he's nothing more that hot air and a suit he hasn't grown into! That's exactly what I fucking *mean*, going to all that effort just to humiliate him when all you needed to do was give him a look — why would you go to the effort? Either you come off as a nonce, or you come off as having taken personally a slight against me that happened months ago, and which *I already dealt with*."

Pike growled wordlessly, dragging his hand back and pacing the room like a tiger in its cage, and Gellert clucked his tongue, rubbing at his neck.

"No one thought that! They thought it was fucking funny, they thought —"

"They're your men, of course they laugh at your jokes and tell you you're scary," Gellert muttered, gesturing widely with one hand. "Have you any idea how pathetic you looked, huge man that you are pinning that young man in your lap, making him sob out his stupid little eyes, for no reason at all? Where's the proportion? Where's the *cause*?"

"He gave me cause," Pike growled, almost swallowing the "v" sound so one barely even heard it. "Came picking a fight —"

"With *me*."

"That's me by extension!"

"So why didn't you just stand up and look down at him?" demanded Gellert. "You saw how scared fucking shitless he was — why didn't you just stare him down? You could have made him cry just doing that, and you'd have looked all the more powerful for it!"

Pike turned to stare at him, wide-eyed and furious.

"You see that I'm right," said Gellert. "This is precisely why they all think you're such an easy target — you're messy, slapdash, disorganised; you have no sense of finesse or restraint. You go a mile when an inch is more than enough, and as you're cheering that no one's gone as far as you have, your competitors are laughing that you've missed out on the prize."

"Four fucking centuries," said Pike in a deep, venomous rumble. "Four fucking centuries, my blood fucking built Lashton, and —"

"And there are *four* rival families, far newer than yours, most of them with just as much territory as you have," said Gellert.

Pike stared at him, jaw dropped, mouth gaping.

"This in't about me at all," he decided after collecting himself, standing up straight. Gellert could the open-mouthed vowel on the second syllable of *about*, heard the way the "t" in at all was swallowed in his throat, *a'all*. Gellert gripped onto these curiosities of pronunciation, different as they were to his own, as though they were rungs of some strange ladder — downward or upward, he didn't have the slightest.

"Oh, *do* tell."

"This is about you getting fondled when *you* was a kid," said Pike.

Gellert, genuinely stunned by that, didn't immediately know how to respond, and Pike rushed to fill the silence.

"I read all them notes they made on you," said Pike. "All that shit about *correcting* your behaviour 'cause you was too autistic, training you like a fucking dog, fucking you about with noise and nagging and taking everything you liked away until you started talking, and I saw them scribbled out bits about *false accusations* once you *could* talk, that shite about you being uncooperative 'cause you didn't jump on his cock when he said how high." Pike was so furious with anger he was spitting wildly, pacing and breathing heavily, all but panting with how furious he was, and the chalky, poreless surface of his vampiric skin had taken on a darker purple tint. "And then when I search it, what do I see but that speech therapist getting done as a nonce before the lung cancer took him out? Bet everyone thought you was an easy target, bet it was non-stop — and it was an open secret that Gwyn Fickle liked girls as young as his cock was long, thirteen his lucky number, but sixteen'd do. That's why you did him, innit, 'cause he tried to fucking fuck you?"

"Yes, Mr Pike," Gellert said in low, dangerous tones, so incredibly angry he was running cold instead of hot. "Because he tried to fucking fuck me."

Pike faltered. "Din't mean you deserved it," he said hurriedly, and Gellert blinked hard. "I just mean —"

"I think," said Gellert, holding up one hand, "that I have had enough of what you *mean* for now."

Pike tried to break the silence twice in the coming minutes, and each time Gellert let out a sharp, hissed noise to make him hush, still collecting himself, and in lieu of expressing himself verbally, Pike went back to pacing the room, worrying his bottom lip with his sharp, protruding teeth.

When Gellert spoke again, Pike froze, turning one ear toward him to listen intently.

"Am I to understand," asked Gellert in a very quiet voice, "that you hired me for this reason?"

"*No*," said Pike. "Just did my fucking research, din't I? And if you're going to act this personal about —"

"It's not personal," Gellert interrupted, as collected as he could be, focusing on the rhythm and intonation of his own voice, carefully polishing every single word. "If you had beaten him or thrown your drink over him or picked him up and thrown him about, I would be making the points I am now."

"But —"

"Shht," hissed Gellert for the third time, and Pike shut his mouth. "In the interests of full transparency," he said slowly, "I did kill Gwyn

Fickle. I was working as a cleaner during the summer in the inn he was staying at. He found me in his room, blocked my way, and tried to reach under my clothes. I shoved him back, he tripped on the curtain — he went over the balcony. Even a skull as thick as his cracks on the cobbles with a four-storey drop."

Pike opened his mouth, and when Gellert looked at him, his lips closed shut again.

"My speech therapist *was* physically abusive. People can have their arguments about applied behavioural therapy, but in my opinion my behavioural therapist was also physically abusive, albeit not sexually so."

"He's dead too," said Pike.

"Yes, I know," said Gellert. "Heart attack, two failed attempts at a bypass, very painful way to go. Do not *ever* presume again to link any attempt I make to corral your temper to abuses made against me in my childhood. Do you understand?"

"You can't tell me what to think," said Pike.

"I'm not trying to," said Gellert. "I *can* tell you not to fucking insult me. You remarked when you hired me that I'm a proud bitch — that is true. And I will not *stand*, Mr Pike, to be moulded, in your eyes, into some sort of exhibit of trauma — particularly not in cases of avid and blatant projection."

"No one touched me up when I was a kid." Pike's anger was a cold, congealed thing. "I in't projecting shit," he said.

"Aren't you?" asked Gellert. "Most men know a mirror when they see one, Mr Pike."

Pike walked past him, and Gellert watched him as he dropped heavily back into his chair, sliding the heels of his hands down its arms, leaning right back against the leather seat.

"You really think I came off like that?" he asked. "Not controlled?"

"Yes," said Gellert. "Although that we appeared to argue over it will draw people's attention, I expect, and people will discuss it. I doubt Dai Laithe will tell people what I said to you, or what you said to me, but people saw me escort him back to his siblings, even if they didn't see you hold him in your lap. It makes it seem more deliberate, that I handed him back rather than forcing them to intervene."

"It used to be easy," muttered Pike. "Now all this computer shit, phones, numbers. So fucking hard just to run the new factory without getting everything undercut."

"The fundamentals of business remain the same, Mr Pike," said Gellert. "Supply, demand."

"Nah," said Pike. "It in't that simple anymore. World's too big, too complicated. You can't just sell what people want — you gotta make 'em want it first, and undercut everyone else." He spoke in a low, miserable voice. "I used to be on top."

"Oh, enough with the self-pity," said Gellert irritably. "You still *are* on top, you pathetic fool. The Kings, the Laithes, the Renns, the Sorrels, they're all scared fucking shitless of you. None of them would try to kill you — most of them wouldn't even dare kill one of your children, no matter how numerous they are."

"You think I'm a brute?" asked Pike.

"Yes, of course I do," said Gellert.

Pike glared at him.

"We are what we are, Mr Pike," said Gellert. "There's no sense in denying the facts."

"Come here," said Pike, and Gellert took a few steps forward, until Pike put his hands on Gellert's hips and gripped at them, sliding his thumbs against Gellert's belly, the divots of his hips, through his shirt. "You fuck?"

"Yes," said Gellert. Pike's hands were large and cold and heavy where they touched him, and there was something grounding in their weight, in their tight grip, in how sold they felt. There was something grounding, too, in Pike's knees either side of Gellert's own.

"When?"

"When I feel like it."

"When'd you last?"

"Before you hired me."

"Yeah," said Pike. "I know *that*."

"You know it wasn't recently, then," said Gellert softly. "Do you have your men keep a little book of my comings and goings when they watch me in my off-hours, make sure I'm not fucking anyone you don't approve of?"

"I won't approve of anyone," said Pike, and grabbed Gellert's cunt through his tailored trousers, making him hiss at the sudden, direct pressure, the slide of Pike's thumb against the nub of his cock through the fabric. "You can tell me you don't want me fucking this cunt all you want, but until I do, no one else is fucking it either."

Pike's fingers were pressing and dragging at Gellert's slit through the trousers, thumb tapping and rubbing against Gellert's cock, and Gellert felt suddenly so drawn tight and turned on he couldn't stand it, his skin fiery with want and *need,* but he didn't put his hands on Pike's shoulders, didn't touch him back just yet.

"Am I supposed to be flattered by a siege?" asked Gellert.

"Don't give a fuck whether you're flattered or not," said Pike. "You work for me. We're not fucking friends, and I'm not your fucking boyfriend. If I want to fuck you, I will."

"Rape me then," said Gellert. "See how efficient it makes me."

Pike made a sound of disgust, dragging his hands back, and Gellert dipped away to lean against the edge of the desk.

"Why are you so convinced I want to fucking rape you?" Pike demanded. "What d'you fucking take me for?"

"You forget the performance I just witnessed?"

"I wasn't gonna fucking rape him," said Pike, scoffing. "I was just getting a reaction out of him."

"By assaulting him."

Pike clucked his tongue, crossing his arms over his chest and shaking his head.

"And me?"

"What about you?"

"Grabbing me through my clothes?"

"You want me to stop, you can make me," said Pike. "But you want me to."

"And if I only want you to because you starve me of all other options?"

"That's want, innit?"

"That's what we call *coercion*, Mr Pike."

"Alright," said Pike, raising his eyebrows. "Then I'll fucking coerce you."

"You don't see how coercion is a breach of consent?"

Pike stared at him very blankly, his face a mask of utter incomprehension. "You're saying it's rape," he said, "if I stop other men fucking you, and then fuck you myself?"

Gellert sighed. "We'll get there, Mr Pike," he said, and splayed his hand on Pike's chest, using the well-oiled wheels of his chair to push him back from the desk, the better for him to pull Pike's keyboard forward and start typing.

It was, he had noted over time, primarily women that Pike interested himself in. Pike liked all manner of women, and would frequently comment on their appearance as if Gellert was about to agree or make any comment at all one way or the other. Pike would comment on their breasts, their arses, their thighs, their faces.

It had become very obvious in the first few months of his new employment that Mr Pike's frequently pregnant employees were not coincidental, and nor were they entirely a result of Pike's general opposition to contraception.

He *liked* to get people pregnant.

More than liked it — it was a fetish. Other people commented on it, within the old hospital, other people in the family — and the fact that there was such a big family was in itself, Gellert thought, a clue.

Pike liked how people looked when they were pregnant, liked their swollen bellies, their chests, their arses and waists, but it wasn't just the physical changes. It was the fertility, too, or at least, the appeal of his own fertility, the thought of his own potency.

Not infrequently, Gellert overheard long conversations between Pike and women with whom he was currently or previously acquainted, often about the size, weight, and general fullness of his bollocks.

That he couldn't impregnate Gellert did not seem at all to have deterred him in his attraction.

"Take your trousers off," said Pike.

Gellert, bent over the desk, said, "No."

"I in't gonna touch you. I just want to see your cunt."

"Yes, your reasons for asking were not unclear. The answer is still no."

Pike sighed, pushing a lever on his chair and dropping the seat's angle so that Pike was laid back. "Will you get in a tizzy if I wank myself off?"

"I don't believe I am in a tizzy," said Gellert. He leaned further forward, so that his suit blazer rode up, that Pike could better see the curve of his arse. "And nor can I stop you from touching yourself in your own office."

He didn't turn to look as he heard Pike breathe heavier, heard the sound of his spit hitting his own palm, heard the wet slip and quiet slap of his hand in his trousers.

"If even a drop lands on me," said Gellert, "I'll burn the whole of the factory downstairs to cinders before I burn you too."

"Understood," Pike grunted, and Gellert passed him a tissue from the box on his desk.

* * *

It was a month later that Gellert left the hospice with a book under his arm. It was a piece of historical fiction, one that his mother had recently been reading with Raquel, one of the guards assigned to her by Pike. Raquel was one of Pike's daughters, was nearly two-hundred years old, and his mother had been all exhausted smiles, saying how funny it was listening to her nitpick about all the errors in it whenever she read aloud.

She'd been very much enjoying the additional, interesting attendants, in the past few weeks, and regularly asked Gellert to pass on her thanks to Pike, which he never did.

Dandy King was outside, one of his hands in his pockets and the other fiddling with a pocket watch, and Gellert came to a stop in front of him, his briefcase held neatly at his side, an umbrella in his other hand, although it didn't look as though he'd need it.

The drizzle from earlier in the afternoon had given way to uncertain sun.

"Is this what you always wanted?" asked Dandy. He was holding his watch, but he wasn't swinging it: he had gathered its chain loosely around his fingers, was squeezing now and then to squeeze the links against his skin. "You could have asked me."

"For what?" asked Gellert.

"I hear your name," said Dandy softly, "whispered on street corners. Comes up in meetings, comes up in conversation. People say Lucien Pike and they say your name as if it's an extension of his. Not even six months, and you're his shadow. Not to everyone, not just yet, but people know you. Know you as an extension of him. Is that what you wanted? From me, from Courageous?"

"No," said Gellert honestly. "I just like what I like, Mr King — work that satisfies me, work that occupies me. Not to mention, of course, that I'm a people person."

Dandy was still for a second, his lips twisting into a small frown, and he looked at Gellert as though he were studying him, searching for any sign that he was joking. Gellert didn't give him one.

"You never seemed like you wanted to be on the map," said Dandy. "I thought you liked it, being in the background."

"I'm still in a background," said Gellert. "I stand behind Mr Pike, in his shadow, as you said."

"What about loyalty?" asked Dandy.

"My loyalty is founded almost entirely on the basis of who will tar and feather me, Mr King, and who will not."

"You say it as if I wanted to," said Dandy, stepping forward, and Gellert shortened his breathing slightly as Dandy came more into his space, if only to spare himself from the painfully overstimulating cloud of Dandy King's subtle cologne. It made him want to cough — funnily enough, it was Mr Pike's vampiric nose that made him so easy to be to close with, when strong colognes had the same effect on him. It was why he scented himself with rosewater and rosewater alone. "You think I wanted to, Gellert?" Dandy's voice was soft, intimate, and he was leaning down slightly so that their noses almost brushed against one another. "It wasn't as if I wanted to see you humiliated, but it had to be done. All those years together — even if we weren't friends, Gellert, I like to think we cultivated a certain working relationship."

"Yes," Gellert agreed. "One that is now at an end."

"Yeah," said Dandy, looking him up and down, and there was a lasciviousness in it that Gellert had seen before, but it was more obvious now, more blatant. His gaze lingered on Gellert's thighs, his waist. The front of his shirt.

Gellert wondered if he felt more territorial over Pike having him than he did over his brother, or less so. Pike lacked the familial spice, the sense of fraternal rivalry, but Pike was a kingpin — it would be a boost for Dandy's ego, thinking he was getting one over on him.

"He fuck you yet?" asked Dandy.

"No," said Gellert.

"He'll get bored of you, once he has," said Dandy softly, leaning forward, and Gellert turned his head to cough quietly, but it made the dryness of his throat from the cologne worse, its pungent sweetness acrid in its own way. "And given as he can't get you pregnant, I don't imagine he'll bother keeping you."

"Hullo, Mr Pike," said Gellert, not turning around, and he watched with interest at the way Dandy's haughty, superior expression, so carefully rehearsed, faltered, and the watch chain went loose in his grip. Dandy's gaze flitted from Gellert's face to Pike behind him.

"How did you know he was there?" whispered Dandy.

"He heard me coming," said Pike. "He does that. Get your fucking hands off him."

"He's not touching me, Mr Pike," said Gellert placatingly, and turned away from Dandy King. Pike waited for Gellert to fall into step with him before the two of them walked out to the car.

"I'll kill him if you fuck him," said Pike.

"Well, that would be very ill-advised," said Gellert. "He's a valued lieutenant of his family, and you can't just mess about with him like you can the likes of Dai Laithe."

"I wouldn't mess about," said Pike. "I'd fucking chop his cock off."

"Again," said Gellert, doing his best to be patient, "there's a certain lacking restraint in your tone, and I don't think it's to anyone's benefit. In any case, I'm not going to fuck him. Dandy only wants to fuck me because my body interests him."

"Interests me, too," said Pike, and Gellert slapped his hand away — it was reflex, at this point.

"It's not quite the same sort of interest," said Gellert, and when Pike held the door open for him, Gellert slipped inside before he did, scooting over in the back seat.

"What's the difference?" asked Pike.

"It's hard to describe," said Gellert. "I'm not sure I could if I tried."

Pike pulled the door shut behind them.

"If he fucks you —"

"He's not going to fuck me, Pike, calm down," said Gellert. "Do you know *why* he wants to fuck me?"

"'Cause you're a cuntboy," said Pike.

"… Astutely and painfully summarised," said Gellert. "Yes, because I'm trans, and because he'd like to win a point against you, but more importantly, because he knows I'm very close to you, and that if he fucked me, he might get access to your stock and distribution. He kept talking about loyalty."

"You're loyal to me," said Pike, raising his voice, and Gellert looked at him sideways, so that Pike crossed his arms over his chest. "Yeah. Well. Pisses me off." He huffed out a frustrated breath. "Can I ask you something?"

"Would you accept my answer if I told you no?"

Pike frowned. "Are you saying no?"

"No," said Gellert.

"Why din't you go to a fleshturner?"

Gellert didn't answer right away as Yves started the winding route out of the hospital car park.

"D'you hear me?" asked Pike.

"Yes, I heard you," said Gellert.

"Hundreds of years," said Pike. "People like you've gone to a fleshturner. Safe. Don't hurt as much. No scars. You din't do that — you went to mundies, let 'em cut you open, cut out the bits you din't want. All that recovery time, bandages, dressing, and you din't need to. Fleshturner could've done it easy as anything — even if you'd have to pay, the Kings would've paid for you, wouldn't they?"

"I don't like fleshturners," said Gellert.

"You seen one before?"

"Part of my therapy," said Gellert. "Do you know what stimming is?"

"When you rub your cock up against some other bloke's."

"No, that's frotting."

"When it's two cunts?"

"Tribbing. Still no — *don't* get distracted, Mr Pike," said Gellert when he opened his mouth to try again. "Self-stimulatory behaviours — everyone does them. Bouncing your leg, rocking in your chair, flapping your hands, popping your lips or your tongue, rubbing fabric. It's stigmatised, in autistic children, in part because of our comparative severity, although mostly because everything about us is stigmatised. In my case, I was overwhelmed by noise, scents. Lights. People constantly fucking *demanding* that I..." He exhaled irritably, tapping his fingers twice, and only twice, against his knee. "I banged my head, slapped my thighs, screamed sometimes. Spun in circles for what seemed like hours. It just made me feel more balanced, less..."

Pike was looking at him, attention utterly focused on Gellert's face.

"They were worried about my development," said Gellert. "It was a short-lived program, corrected the problem — an autistic child being too autistic — without having to address the cause — an unwelcoming and overstimulating environment."

"He made you less sensitive?" asked Pike. "What, plugged your ears and softened your brains?"

"Oh no," said Gellert, with a bitter laugh. "No, that's not the point of ABA. I'm as sensitive as I ever was. The fleshturner would forcibly relax some of my joints, my body. Turn the nerve endings off like they were light switches — temporary, limited paralysis. If I screamed, he'd reach into my throat and make it so I couldn't anymore."

Pike's expression was one of cold, hard fury.

"Yes," said Gellert. "Very upsetting, I know. I told you it was a short-lived program — the fleshturner that involved himself in it, he was quite riddled with guilt afterwards, as you can imagine. Torturing a child until he learned not to scream anymore didn't sit well with him."

"Does it still hurt?" asked Pike.

"Sometimes."

Pike was looking out of the window, wasn't looking directly at Gellert. He kept looking at Gellert in the reflection in the glass — he did that, sometimes, oscillated between very direct, very aggressive eye contact, and no eye contact at all.

"It got worse for me," he said. "When I got turned. Makes everything more sensitive, your eyes, your ears, your sense of smell. Freaked out when they invented the steam engine. Fucked me up, the noise it made — the fucking, uh, the whistle from the steam, the pistons. I could hear the little creaks and rusty noises whenever the cogs wasn't oiled right. Din't have a car for ages neither, not 'til they made 'em quieter."

"If it's any consolation —"

"The fuck do I need consoling for?"

"Well, you look glum, and it's pathetic," said Gellert. "As I was saying, if it's any consolation, you provide a very comfortable working environment. Dim lights, relative quiet, no strong scents."

"Why's it pathetic that I give a fuck?" asked Pike.

"Because no one else does, Mr Pike," said Gellert.

"D'you know what's not pathetic?"

"Is it your penis?"

"Yeah."

"Agree to disagree," said Gellert, and Pike scoffed.

"Good distraction, cures a migraine," said Pike. "Cold compress, and an orgasm. They'd bottle me and sell me if they could."

"Devastatingly evocative imagery," said Gellert, "but I don't have a migraine."

"Preventative measure," said Pike.

Gellert patted his knee. "No, Mr Pike," he said.

Mr Pike slumped back in his seat. "How's your mum?" he asked.

"Good," said Gellert. "She's very good."

* * *

"There's something to be said for the double standard, you know," said Gellert, and Pike turned to look at him, seeming confused.

"Huh?"

"You keep advising me that if I fuck anybody, you will in some way mutilate and/or murder him."

"Oh," said Pike, and then, without shame, "Yeah."

"And yet you are near constantly fucking women, and sometimes other men," said Gellert.

"That's your fault, innit?" asked Pike.

Gellert arched an eyebrow. "Go on."

"Not doing your job," said Pike. "You warm my cock, let me fuck you, I won't need to go for anyone else. If my cock is satisfied, I don't need to leave my fucking office. Ergo, s'your fault I fuck other people."

"... *Ergo*?"

"I din't use it right?"

"No, no, you did. Just not a word I've heard you use before."

"You're rubbing off on me."

"Evidently."

"You can rub off on me," Pike offered. "I've got nice thighs to rub on."

"Your cock isn't nice to rub on?"

"It is. Why, do you wanna...?"

"No."

"Tease."

"What happens, Mr Pike, if I let you fuck me, and I find you disappointing?"

"I keep going 'til you're not disappointed," said Pike, as though it were obvious. "Just 'cause my balls are dry don't mean I can't use my tongue and my fingers."

The confidence he said it with, clean and blunt and utterly unflinching, was in its own way, deeply appealing. It was irritating that it was appealing — Pike had a habit of subtly sniffing the air, his nostrils flaring visibly, whenever he managed to turn Gellert on, and he did this now, his red-brown eyes lighting up.

"Does it bother you," Gellert asked, "that you wouldn't be able to get me pregnant?"

"I'd fucking love to get you pregnant," Pike said immediately, and Gellert felt his nose wrinkle. "I know I *can't*. It'd just... You'd be fit. Pregnant. Full of me. All square and stern as you are, made round instead, and not able to forget what done it, who done it. Waddling around all slow, thighs wide, inviting everyone to come fuck you again just by standing."

This was more of an insight into Pike's psyche than Gellert had been prepared for, though it was undoubtedly what he'd asked for, and it was his own fault for asking. "And the resulting infant?"

"Why do you care so much about fucking babies?"

"It's not that I care about babies, Mr Pike, it's that when you're so focused on breeding everyone you lay eyes on, you have to remain cognizant of the result. All these bastards of yours, but I've nary seen you hold a baby or bounce a child on your knee — all of your children I see are adults, each and all of them treated the same as any other of those you have employed."

"What about it?" demanded Pike. He didn't like to be questioned on matters like these ones, became defensive, curled his lips, got all sour of mood, and he was doing this now, fidgeting in his chair. "S'a crime not to like kids now, is it? As if the world's gonna fucking end 'cause I don't wanna babysit?"

"It's not babysitting when it's your own children, Mr Pike. It's just parenthood."

Pike sucked his teeth.

"Why do you like it so much?" asked Gellert. "Pregnancy. You're obsessed."

"S'natural, innit?" asked Pike.

"No," replied Gellert. "Not like you do it. Have you ever been married?"

Pike scoffed. "No."

"How many children do you have?"

Pike shrugged his shoulders.

"Alright," said Gellert. "When you were born? Sixteenth century?"

"I don't fucking know," muttered Pike. "We din't exactly get birth certificates back then."

"How many do you impregnate in a year?"

"As many as I feel like."

"Two this year so far."

"Three," said Pike.

"That many every year? Since you were, what, twenty-five? Or did this preoccupation start earlier? Later? Only when you were turned?"

"What's it fucking matter?"

"What does it matter? Well, at a loose and conservative estimate, you've likely fathered over a thousand children."

"Yeah," said Pike.

"Grandchildren?"

"Yeah."

"Great grandchildren?"

"Prob'ly."

"You mean you don't know?"

Pike looked at him very, very sourly, and then said, "Two birds with one stone if you just let me fuck you. No womb, no risk."

"You're a natural debater, Mr Pike," said Gellert.

"Meeting tonight at nine," said Pike, and Gellert frowned, sliding his hand over to the datebook on Pike's desk. "Nah, don't write it down. Some young lad joined the factory staff downstairs. Don't know who he belongs to. Gonna find out."

"Oh," said Gellert. "We're interrogating him?"

"That bother you?"

"No," said Gellert. "Why would it?"

"I might torture him," said Pike.

Gellert met Pike's gaze, unimpressed, and retorted, "So might I."

Pike, quite unsubtly, adjusted the bulge in his trousers, and Gellert's lips twitched as he turned back to his work.

* * *

He supposed it was inevitable that he was kidnapped.

They drugged him to do it, caught him as he was finished running papers to one of their accountants and pushed a soaked cloth over his mouth and nose, the sort of thing a man couldn't resist no matter how stubborn he was. When he woke, it was with a loose hood over his head, without his glasses, and his wrists very loosely tied.

He was alone in a room, dank, stone, cold — a cellar.

The young man they'd caught in the factory the month previous had not, it turned out, been a native of Lashton — not a Renn or a Sorrel, nor a King or a Laithe. He'd come up from down south on the coast, was due to bring back knowledge of the factory's running so that its success might be replicated.

It was almost impossible to grow fae mushrooms of the sort needed for pixie dust without being deep in fae country — Gellert had no idea of their Latin names, and Mr Pike referred to the varieties exclusively by colourful and filthy eponyms Gellert refused to believe were official names in any capacity — but they had managed the conditions in the cellar by working closely with a few highly qualified wizards and fae mycologists, and it was no surprise that the techniques used were the subject of great interest.

They weren't even a gang, not really — or if they were, they were the offshoot of a larger organisation, given a sort of freedom to keep them out of the hair of everybody else.

Gellert suspected this in large part because the bondage keeping him in place was so shoddy it need not have been there at all.

Shifting up on his feet where he was sitting on the floor, he passed his wrists under his arse, his legs, until his tied hands were in front of him. The zip ties were loose enough that it only took two tries to bring his arms down hard against his knees before they snapped apart.

"Amateurs," Gellert muttered, and pulled the hood from over his head, as if it made any difference to his sight in the dim light, blurry as everything was.

He felt his way to the cellar stairs and found the door at the top of the stairs not even locked — it opened into a hall, and fumbling on the ground, he found his bag right outside the door.

It was almost offensive, frankly. Insulting, in a way.

He knew where his proper glasses were — they were on Pike's desk, because one of the arms had come loose and Pike had fixed them with a tiny screwdriver. He'd been wearing a set of spares, of which he now had half a dozen, until they'd been dragged off him.

His spare knife, of course, was exactly where it ought be.

He almost convinced himself, imagined to himself, that it was some sort of trick, that he had not actually been captive by some idiot students of drug production at all, but that this was just a gambit to lull him into a false sense of security by the Kings, perhaps.

This hope faded when he found every one of his captors crammed into the same room, watching *Shrek*.

"Man, he seemed pretty pissed on the phone," said one of them — he sounded young. Gellert couldn't well see them, but there were half a dozen of them, and the room was thick with strong scents and perfumes. "You sure we should have taken this guy?"

"We just need to know how it works, how they map everything out," said one of the others. "It's not like we're going to threaten their *market*, is it? I mean, they can't expect Lashton to be the only centre of production outside of fae realms."

Gellert narrowed his eyes.

"We're not going to hurt him, anyway," said another. "Just hold him 'til he tells us something, or swap him for the info we need. If Pike was that attached, this guy would have a bodyguard."

"Maybe he doesn't need one," said the first one, and all of them laughed.

Gellert crept silently back to the front door of the little flat they were in, temporary lodgings that were mostly unfurnished, and locked it shut.

* * *

"Come pick me up," he said into one of their phones. His own was lost, dropped outside of the accountant's, but all of them had had phones, expensive, sleek things.

Pike was half asleep — it was very late by now — and grunted incoherently.

Gellert wasn't in the mood to argue with him, nor to raise his voice, and instead, he employed a distasteful technique he well knew would work: making his voice as breathless and as sultry as he could manage, he said, "*Daddy*, will you come get me?"

He almost imagined he could see Pike straightening in bed like he was spring-loaded.

"Who's this?" he demanded, abruptly wide awake.

"It's Gellert," he said, dropping the voice. "Come get me."

"You was kidnapped," said Pike, but Gellert could hear his clothes shuffling in the background.

"Ask someone to run me a bath, and ask Yves if he could put a tarpaulin on the backseat, would you? I know he hates getting blood in his car, and I'm... messy."

"Glasses?"

"Would be helpful, yes."

An hour later, Pike sat on the closed lid of the toilet and watched Gellert bathe. He'd stood under the hot water of the shower in the poky little flat before he'd walked out to the car, and therefore his bathwater was only slightly pink instead of gooey and red.

"You din't have to kill them all," said Pike.

"I know," said Gellert. "I could have left one alive, but I lost my temper. You're familiar with that, aren't you?"

"D'you like hurting people?" asked Pike. He was looking at Gellert with interest — he'd helped him undress, and he'd looked at Gellert's body with a curiosity that was surprisingly lacking in lasciviousness, touching the moles at the divot of his hip before he reached and carefully brushed one of his chest scars with his fingers. Now, his gaze was not on Gellert's body, on the scars at his chest or his gut, on the hair or the slight jut of his cock between his legs, but on Gellert's hands as he scrubbed himself clean.

"Not especially," said Gellert. "But I don't dislike it, and I more than see its value as deterrent. These people don't understand Lashton, which is not a sin, but they also don't respect it, which in my eyes, certainly is. They didn't understand the severity of their actions, nor the severity of potential response. Their people will understand now."

"You don't like southerners," said Pike.

"It's Londoners I don't like," said Gellert, and Pike laughed, a gritty sound. "No, it isn't... It's no sense of northern pride, Mr Pike. I like Lashton — I was made here, forged into what I am. I don't care that outsiders find it messy or brutal: Lashton is my world. They don't need to fit into its machinations if they don't wish to, but I don't care to have these people dip their hands in to take what they like, and claim we never made anything worth taking in the first place."

"It's hot when you get like this," said Pike. "All cold and bloodthirsty."

"You get hot when you look in a mirror, you mean," muttered Gellert.

"You did a sexy voice on the phone."

"I won't be doing it ever again."

Pike came forward, kneeling on the map beside the bath, and Gellert looked at him, the shape of his face, the intent press of his lips together. Pike's was very low as he started, "Can I, uh...?"

He trailed off.

"Can you?" Gellert repeated crisply.

Pike sounded nervous, his jacket rustling as he fidgeted, even if his face didn't entirely show it, although his gaze shifted rapidly from side to side. He put his hands on the bath's sides. Softly, so softly Gellert would have strained to hear it, if not for his own sensitive hearing, Pike asked, "Can I wash your hair?"

Gellert considered this, and then handed Pike his glasses. "Yes," he said. "If you like."

Pike's big hands were cold, but the water was still comfortably hot, and his fingers were very gentle as he began to lather shampoo into Gellert's hair, massaging his scalp in the process. Gellert closed his eyes, humming and relaxing into Pike's keen and careful grip.

"You're very good at this," said Gellert.

"Thanks," said Pike, slightly fast, almost as though he was shy about it.

"This is a fetish of yours you don't indulge as often as the others, I assume?"

"Not a fetish," said Pike, and brought a jug of water over his head, pouring it over Gellert's hair and rinsing it through. "I can wash hair for the same reason I can fix your glasses and pull out teeth. My dad was a barber."

"Your mother?"

"None of your business," said Pike, which was in its way, no real surprise.

Gellert leaned right into Pike's hands, went limp in the water and let Pike moved him as he wanted to, pressing his fingers so hard into Gellert's scalp in places that it ached in a dull, panging way, and then sent warmth and slackness all through Gellert's body, running down his spine before making its home in his limbs. Pike conditioned his hair, once it was washed.

Pike didn't try to wash the rest of Gellert's body, didn't reach to touch him, but when he stood to his feet, Pike rushed to towel him off. Gellert thought it was ridiculous, but he let it happen, let Pike focus himself on rubbing the towel over every inch of Gellert's skin, massaging him in the process.

"You're wet," he observed. "Smells good."

"You've been carefully rubbing my body for some half an hour," said Gellert. "Are you surprised I'm wet?"

"No," said Pike, and Gellert didn't need his glasses to know that he was half-grinning. "You think I'm fit."

Gellert sighed. He did his best to sound long-suffering, as if he was annoyed, trying to hide the eager thrill that burned under his skin. He was hot and sensitive, arms aching from fighting and wrestling with knives, no matter that the bath had soothed him.

"If you must," he said at length, leading the way from the bathroom and into the bedroom, Pike following behind him. "Careful with those teeth."

"Fuck yes," said Pike, and shoved Gellert hard onto the bed, dropping face first between his legs.

* * *

The next afternoon, Gellert was on his feet and taking notes as Pike conducted an idle interview with a contact on some Saes authority — it wasn't the police, but some smuggling patrol with a ridiculous name, even more worthy of scorn than the cops themselves.

Pike dragged Gellert closer to the desk, and without asking, without even faltering in his offer of terms to the officer on the phone, he bent Gellert over, dragging his trousers down and standing behind him.

Gellert, bemused but not all that surprised — it was no surprise to learn that Pike was as bored of this carry-on as he was — braced his elbows on the desk and swapped to a pen that wouldn't smudge.

If the sound of flesh slapping against flesh bothered the patrol officer on the other end of the line, they didn't mention it. They were probably used to this from Pike.

Even as Pike sped up, neither of them moaned — or at least, Gellert didn't.

When Gellert took one of Pike's big hands from his hips and repositioned it to settle on the back of his neck, a silent demand for Pike to pin him down, Pike let out a throaty, eager noise which he politely ignored but was, frankly, an embarrassment.

Gellert told him so as soon as they were done.

FIN.

More from the Author

If you'd like to seek out more of my work, *Heart of Stone* is a full-length novel set in the 18th century, and is a slowburn slice-of-life romance between a vampire and his secretary, the vampire ADHD and the secretary autistic. It has a lot of humour and domestic elements throughout.

My most recent release, *Powder and Feathers*, is a long-form contemporary dark romance with a great many fantasy elements, featuring a fucked-up dynamic between a Fallen angel and a depressed artist he begins stalking in the park.

If you're interested in perusing more novella-length pieces and short stories, I publish a huge variety of short stories that are available on a subscription model from Patreon[1] or as part of your Medium[2] subscription!

I normally publish at least one new piece a week, whether that's short stories, longer form short stories like this one, serial updates for my chaptered works, or non-fiction pieces like essays and analyses.

My name is Johannes T. Evans on both sites.

My website: www.JohannesTEvans.com[3]

My Twitter: @JohannesTEvans[4]

And finally, if you'd like to get regular email updates from me, with media recommendations, links to my most recently published work, and other little announcements, you can sign up at www.buttondown.email/JohannesTEvans.

---

1.   https://www.patreon.com/JohannesEvans

2.   https://johannestevans.medium.com/directory-of-work-6291c6e102b9

3.   http://www.JohannesTEvans.com

4.   https://twitter.com/johannestevans

Also by Johannes T. Evans

Lashton Town
Gellert's New Job
Daddy's Boy
A King's Man
King's Sentence

Standalone
Heart of Stone
In Perpetuity
Scattered Stories (Short Story Compilation)
The Mermaid and the Fisherman
Divine Service
Gerald Poole and the Pirates
Powder and Feathers
Cold Comfort
More Than Coffee
Touch-Starved
Divine Bodies
Fallen Dust
Hunger at Sea
The Angel in the Woods
Archival Management

The Widower's Garden
Au Naturale
The Lord of the Wood's Spring Bride
Agony and Ecstasy
Sleeping Beauty
Sweet On
A Gift for the Wolfmen
The Stasis Box
Saint Jude's Kitchen
Alexander's Angel
Ambitious Men
Remnants of a Bygone Era
Dirk and the Weaver
Unlikely Matches
Like A Thief and an Assassin
Deep Breath
Good Coin
Agreements and Curses
Bone-Eater, Hungry for Fire
The Devil's Mark
The Many Deaths of Baldr the Undying
For Want of Time
Room for Dessert
Paper Houses
Steps Ahead
Hitting the Books
Workplace Connections